C. VONZALE LEWIS

DESCENDANTS OF THE BIG HOUSE

C. VONZALE LEWIS

Book Layout

Edited by Carla Lewis, Jess Moore

Cover Art and Design © 2024 Adina Chiles

Interior Formatting by Book Savvy Services

Johnson, Georgia Douglas. "Foredoom", *The Heart of a Woman*, 1918

Content Warning; Depictions of Suicide.

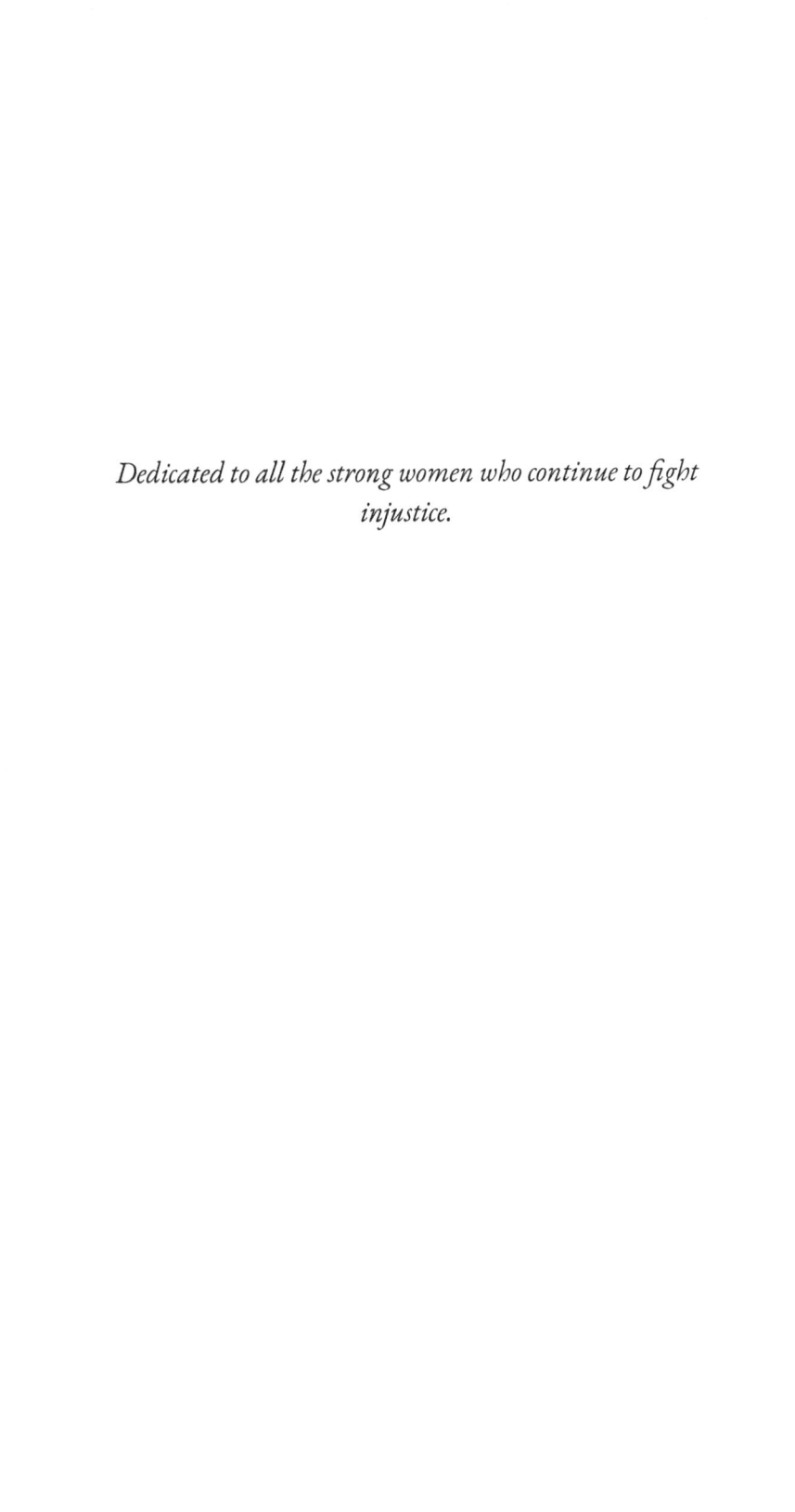

Dedicated to all the strong women who continue to fight injustice.

We shall overcome because the arc of the moral universe is long, but it bends toward justice.
–Dr. Martin Luther King Jr., "Remaining Awake Through a Great Revolution." Speech given at the National Cathedral, March 31, 1968.

Dear Reader,

I've never added a content warning to any of my stories. For me, the title, blurb, and genre would have been warning enough. But for this story, it's not evident in the title.

I needed a warning when writing this. There are some deeply troubling elements that I've never wanted to dig into. Mostly dealing with the cruelty my ancestors had to endure. For some, like me, these topics would be too much. So, I want to caution you in a way that does not give away the story.

The past is rife with injustice and cruelty. I touch on these things a bit. But the present is also filled with its troubles because human cruelty is forever present in our daily life. If you have trouble reading about hatred and the many ways in which women can be mistreated, then I advise you to read no further.

If you do decide to continue reading, I hope you find some sliver of hope in this story.

Sincerely,
C. Vonzale Lewis

Her life was dwarfed, and wed to blight,
Her very days were shades of night,
Her every dream was born entombed,
Her soul, a bud, —that never bloomed.

Georgia Douglas Johnson
"Foredoom"

THE PLEASANT FAMILY

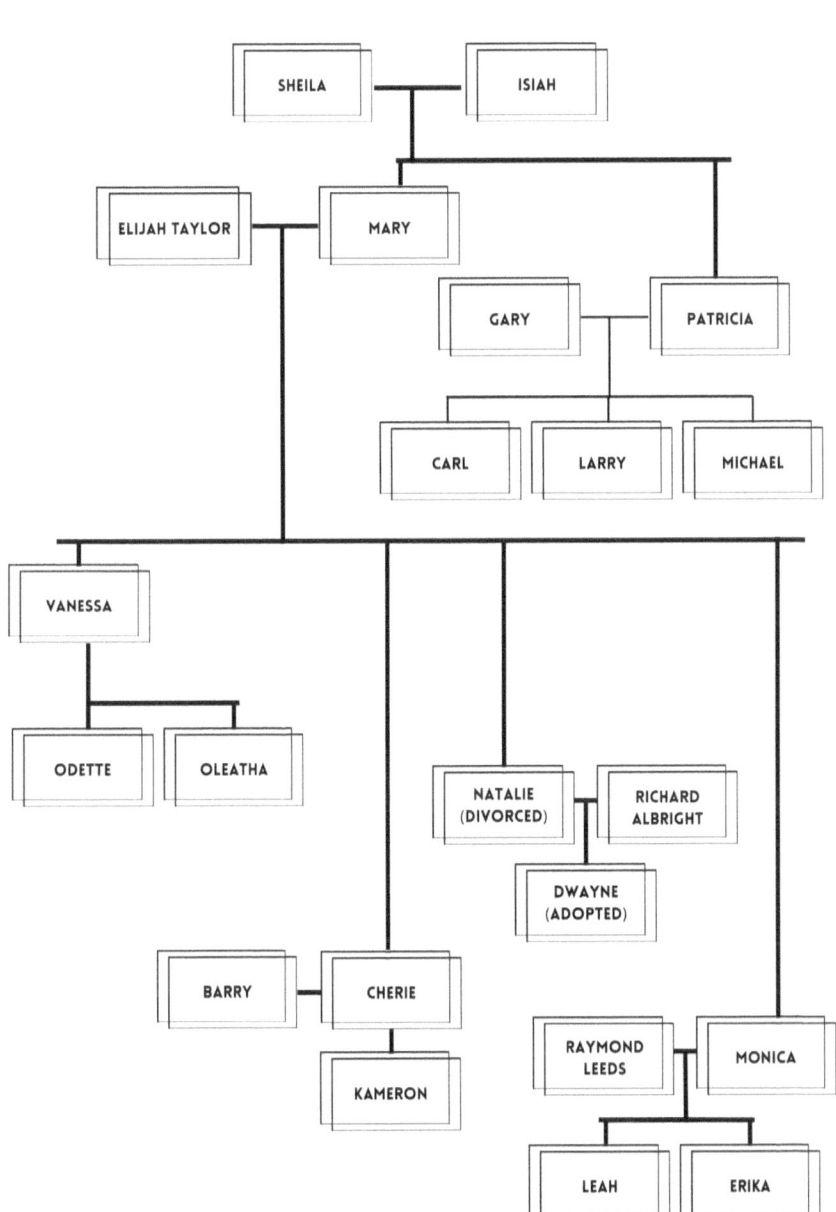

Contents

One

The middle of our one-room precinct, sitting across from my partner Raphael Sinclair at our shared desk, was the wrong place to be obsessed with learning about my lineage. There was no privacy in this small space. Only the chief had the illusion of such with her glass-enclosed office on the opposite side of our open-floor breakroom.

At any moment one of the other three detectives could find my feverish study of the journal I held in my hand more interesting than the case they were supposed to be reviewing.

But I didn't care. I was too caught up in a snare of discovery and sense of betrayal.

A spasm of pain shot down my legs. The knot just above my tailbone throbbed. Dryness clawed at the back of my throat. But I ignored all of it. And just kept reading.

We are lost in the midst of imbalance. I shall find the point of intersection.

BALANCE
~~I will kill all the good and save all the evil and still it won't work.~~
NO NO NO NO. GOOD MUST WIN. NOT EVIL.
THERE IS NO BALANCE

"There is no balance," I whispered, trying out the words written in the journal and searching my mind for the meaning missing from the page. Had she given up trying to find the balance? Or had she concluded there wasn't a way to keep it?

"What?" my partner, Raphael, asked.

"Nothing," I said and finally picked up my coffee and took a drink. The creak of the rotating ceiling fan needled at my nerves. They still hadn't repaired our air-conditioning. Nervous energy sent electric pinpricks along my bare arms, making me flush.

Last weekend, I'd started to clean the attic in my childhood home. It wasn't the first time since my mother's passing five years ago that cleaning out the house became my priority. And each time I tried, I always ended up with piles of stuff I could never give away. Too much history in those walls. Both good and bad. The bad memories kept me from ever living there. A promise to my dying mother kept me from selling it.

All the women on my mother's side of the family had kept journals. Some filled with love and adventure and others filled with their own variations of the practices and rituals passed down from my 5th great grandma, Felicia LaRue, who lived in the house in the late 1800s. Most of her earlier journals were dedicated to her craft. Over the years, her entries had grown darker and more fatalistic in nature. Like something or someone had corrupted her soul. But it never spoke of specifics regarding what had caused this shift in her being.

I'd made a home for the journals I could display on a bookshelf, handcrafted by a local carpenter, and had arranged them by date. My one contribution to the home, aside from the yearly maintenance and overall upkeep of the place. It made me feel more like a caretaker than a previous occupant of the house.

And now, I had to find a place for the diaries I'd recently found buried in a box of sewing material, bound together with red velvet fabric. Because these could not go on display. While the dark content reminded me of Grandma Felicia's journals, these ramblings were much more and everything to do with the torment and cruelty of being a Champion for Good and Evil.

During Mardi Gras earlier this year, I'd met the human embodiment of evil. He called himself Papa Sin. And after helping me solve a case in which he was directly involved, he told me I was a Champion for Good and Evil. And six months later, I still had no idea what that enormous title entailed.

I kneaded the small of my back with my fist, trying to work out a knot. I'd been hunched over for what seemed like hours now, furiously reading each page with a single-minded determination to find answers to my dilemma.

The first in this series of journals written by my grandma Lucille had already shown signs of her mind breaking. Incoherent thoughts intermingled with details of people she encountered. Individuals she had judged to be either good or evil and the small influences she'd had on their lives. She sounded like a master manipulator—whispering in a person's ear—swaying them one way or the other. All to restore balance. At least that's what she had written about herself.

I convinced him to kill his friend. It was the only way to restore balance.

My memories of my grandmother had always been filled with joy and happiness. She'd come to live with us after my father's death. The abuse my mother and I had endured for years had been kept from her, and she spent her last days helping us heal. Now, those memories were tainted with the knowledge of all the twisted things she had done.

Would I become like her?

There had to be more journals, ones she began when she first met Papa Sin and Mama Root. Right? I kept going back to that thought. Yet every search since had yielded no results. The frustration of it was wearing on me.

"Learn anything?" Raphael asked abruptly.

"Well," I said with a sigh, looking across the desk at him. "I might end up going crazy."

Raphael tilted his head to the side. "We won't let that happen."

I gave him a quick smile and looked away. I wish he could stop my eventual descent into madness. Because despite only seeing two instances of my ancestor's struggle with mental health, I knew they all had. I just hadn't found all the proof yet.

The precinct phone rang, pulling everyone's attention. "Silverwood Police Department. How may I direct your call?" Our receptionist looked at us, then after a beat, frowned and shook her head. "No, Mrs. Clark, they haven't moved the grocery store. Is Billy around?"

The Silverwood, Georgia police department had five detectives and twenty patrol officers for the twenty-seven thousand residents, most of whom were well into the senior years. We had our share of crime but most of it occurred during and after the tourist season.

On days like this, Chief Declouette had us going through what she'd dubbed as the 'Fresh Eyes' review. Old cases were brought out and exchanged between the five detectives to see if we could find any new leads. No one liked that sort of scrutiny of their work.

My partner Raphael and I were looking through an old hit and run. My quick read-through let me know we were never going to solve it. The driver wasn't a local. The plates were stolen. And every drunken eyewitness statement read like a fever-dream, with varying degrees of lunacy intertwined. Rarely did we find witnesses who astutely observed what was going on around them. Which meant most statements were filled with fabrications and embellishments with only a kernel of truth thrown in. And it was our job to weed through all of it.

With a heavy sigh, I returned to my own search. And tried not to think about how it was also turning out to be pointless.

The next few pages were more of the same. It was as if Grandma Lucille's mind was slowly deteriorating. Like she was screaming in her head and nobody was listening. One entry was dated the year before she died. All I remember from that time was the joy she had in my college acceptance. I pictured her on the day I left. Mouth stretched wide in a smile, while tears of joy streamed down her face. *"You have somethin' in you that will make you a great officer, my little Beatrice. Somethin' great."*

Now her words held a deeper meaning. She had known what I was and would become one day. Police. Why didn't she warn me? Why didn't she tell me about all the horrific things she had done and the ways in which I might be forced to do the same?

But I wished she'd told us she was suffering.

I turned the page.

This was the end of everything. I read the date. A few weeks before she died, she had covered the page with a single message:

We are born in sin. We are born in sin. We are born in sin.

And the last line:

Just twisted souls upon the Tree of Life.

None of her previous journals had references to Christianity or any other religion, so why was she talking about sin?

I got up and went to the breakroom, needing a minute to think. The coffee was gone, and my throat was still dry. After retrieving a bottle of water from the refrigerator, I cracked the sealed cap, leaned against the counter and sipped— thoughts on that single line.

Just twisted souls upon the Tree of Life.

The first idea that came to mind was puppetry. Our souls like marionettes hung from branches, jerking and dancing until their strings tangled. Was that what Champions were? And what would that make the Tree of Life? The puppeteer, a great manipulator.

I rubbed the knot on my back again, wondering if there would be any point in requesting an ergonomic chair. I needed to move. Do something. All this sitting around couldn't be good for me.

"Well, damn," one of the detectives yelled out. "It's been three months since his execution and seems one of them streaming services is doing a documentary on the Pasadena Butcher."

Everyone groaned. I hated those shows. Always romanticizing and embellishing on the life of some deranged killer for ratings. Completely forgetting about the pain their victims' families endured. In this case, the Butcher had killed over sixty women before he was caught, not by a confession but a selfie one of his victims had sent before her death.

I returned to my desk and sat down heavily in my uncomfortable chair. I might have to buy my own. Raphael spared me a brief glance, then resumed his reading, a smile stretching across his face.

I looked down at the journal again.

We are born in sin. We are born in sin. We are born in sin. Just twisted souls upon the Tree of Life.

"Damnit!" I yelled.

Raphael looked up. "You all right over there?"

I stared at him, shaking my head. "I'm missing something. I know I am."

He just stared at me, his warm brown eyes assessing. "Take a break." A smile slowly stretched across his face. "Look at it with...fresh eyes."

"You are not funny," I said, laughing. "I'm almost done."

"Good. Then we can go grab some lunch at Lewis' Catfish and Po Boys."

"Sounds like a plan."

I flipped through the last few pages, all covered in the same message. My hopes of learning anything more died with each page turned. Something had driven my grandmother to this point of hopelessness. To the point that she stopped trying to find balance and focused all her energy on sin.

I got to the last page of the journal and stopped.

A phantom pain slowly crawled down my spine.

Unable to breathe, I stared at the macabre drawing of The Tree of Life. Its vines were twisted and grotesque. Limbs withered with decay oozing out of the cracks. Done in a realistic style, the ink drawing seemed to pulse with life. I ran my finger along the page and could feel the rough indentations her pencil left on the cream-colored paper. Resting in the thick of brambles and dead leaves were tiny boxes filled with a single phrase.

We are but twisted souls on The Tree of Life.

Something about the tree mesmerized me, as if I were being pulled into the space where it existed on those cream-colored pages. I could almost feel a cool wind caressing my face. Smell the damp soil in which this twisted, majestic oak rested. The branches moved, swaying in the breeze. I lifted my hand and ran a finger along the ridge-covered leaf. Like a message in braille had been imprinted on them. I closed my eyes against the wind and concentrated on what I was feeling.

Just twisted souls upon the tree of life.

My heart pounded in my chest; the sound pulsed against my eardrums. A hollow ache formed in my throat. Raw and unyielding. I swallowed the emotion. The world tilted and filled with a dark pulsing sky. It reminded me of the first time I spotted the Sin Exchange. A way station that sat at the crossroads, connecting the entire world to a single pop-up shop where Mama Root tended her herbs.

"We are born in sin. We are born in sin. We are born in sin," A soft voice chanted in my head. My chest heaved and the image blurred. I was once again sitting rooted in my chair, eyes glued to the image. The ink on the page swirled, the branches forming words...no, names...I touched the page and felt warmth on my fingertips.

"Bee!"

I jerked, and slammed the journal shut—the sound suddenly cutting off. I shook my head and stared across the desk at my partner. His image wavered for a bit; I blinked a few times bringing him into focus.

Before I could show Raphael what I'd found, a commotion broke out at the front of the precinct. I turned and found a woman standing in the lobby with tears in her eyes.

"I'd like to talk to someone about my aunt's murder."

Two

The woman, now talking to Sgt. Dennis in a harsh whisper, seemed familiar. It was as if we had encountered each other sometime in the past, and a significant detail about her had stayed with me subconsciously. Since her aunt lived here, she must have visited Silverwood before, and I'd simply ran into her. No. It was much more than that. A possible witness in a crime I investigated. No, that wasn't it, either.

Tall, with brown skin, she wore her jet-black hair in a tight French braid that trailed down her back. She'd dressed for the weather in a green short-sleeved top with V-shaped neckline, allowing for a hint of cleavage. Cream and gold decorative earrings dangled from her ears and only a faint hint of makeup accented her face.

How did I know her?

I concentrated on her voice. Her Patois had a blend of southern and western inflections, making it difficult to determine where she was from. But if I had to hazard a guess, I'd say she was from out west. Maybe even California. She had what people often described as 'vocal fry'—a low rumbling sound at the end of her sentences.

As she listened to the Sergeant's responses, the look she gave him was laced with scorn and challenge. It reminded me of us southern women. We tended to cut with words and looks. Which meant she either grew up in the south or visited frequently.

Again, where had I seen her before?

"And I'm telling you," she said carefully, voice raising slightly. "She was killed. Now, do I have to come around the desk and assist you with doing your job, or are you going to get someone with more authority and patience to come talk to me?" She paused, let out a long breath. "I've traveled too damn far to get turned away."

"Ma'am," Sergeant Dennis said, his patience sounding a little frayed. A red flush spread across his neck and his back stiffened.

"No. Not ma'am," she said through clenched teeth. "My name, *once again*, is Odette Palmer. You can call me Odette. Ms. Palmer. Mrs. Palmer. None of the ma'am shit.

I'm here to talk to someone about my aunt's death. Get. Someone. Over. Here. Now! You wasted my time on the phone and now you're wasting it here. In person, mind you."

Despite the harshness in her words and manner, there was a vulnerability about her that reminded me of a scared child lashing out and using verbal abuse to hide their fear and vulnerability.

"And I've told you," Sergeant Dennis said, his voice deepening. "Over the phone and now here *in person* that Ms. Albright died of natural causes. Our coroner ruled as such. So, it is." He sighed and sprayed his big, beefy hands on the desk. "I am truly...truly sorry for your loss. But that don't change the circumstances," he said, head shaking. "I wish you had trusted me instead of traveling all 'cross the country for no reason."

"You don't seem to be listening. I can write it down for you if you're having trouble. Or you can get me someone who does have comprehension skills."

"Calm. Down." While he didn't yell the last statement. The attack on his intelligence had gotten his back up. And he knew very well that you should never tell a woman to calm down.

I slipped the journal back into my desk drawer and stood. "We better go handle this," I said and started for the front, trusting my partner to follow.

I stopped just to the right of Dennis and placed a hand on his shoulder. He sighed loudly and turned to me. "This is Ms. Albright's niece, Ms. Odette Palmer." Exacerbation laced his tone. "No need for you to intervene. I have it under control." The tightness around his eyes suggested otherwise.

"Are you a detective?" she asked, turning her dark hazel eyes on me.

They say the eyes are the windows to our souls. It was a deep way of saying that to read a person one must make eye contact. What I saw in Odette Palmer's eyes was sheer terror and pain.

"Yes," I said softly. "I'm Detective Monroe," I glanced over my shoulder. "And this is my partner, Detective Sinclair. Do you need help?"

She nodded, tears welling up in her eyes, and let out a sigh of relief. "Yes," she said, head still going up and down. "Yes." Her shoulders slumped as if all the fight had drained out of her. All she needed was someone to show a little compassion.

Raphael stepped around the desk. "Why don't we go somewhere to talk," he said, reaching for her. She looked up at him and nodded again. He guided her out of the waiting area and toward the hallway leading to our interview rooms.

When they were out of sight, I turned to Seargent Dennis. "What's going on?"

He rubbed the back of his neck. "She called a few days ago, claiming someone killed Ms. Albright. Told her she was mistaken, then she became..." he trailed off, looking a little guilty. "I didn't handle it too well. I'll admit that. But Beatrice, you know. We get all kinds callin' in here claiming this that and the other. I tried to be sympathetic." He flung his hand toward the hallway. "But you seen how she acted."

I didn't respond. His accusatory tone got under my skin. While the woman had been a little abrasive, I didn't believe for a second she'd started off that way. Sgt. Dennis had a way of getting under a person's skin. Old school and not afraid to use colorful language when he wanted to. He was bullish and stuck in his ways and really didn't like anyone contradicting him. But under all of that bluster was a really good officer. He knew his job. He just wasn't keen on adapting to any new avenues of policing.

The chief had been trying to get him to retire, but the man refused to leave.

"Well. We'll talk to her now," I said, staring at him. "Might have helped when she called as well."

He frowned. "I didn't see..."

I shook my head, cutting off his next words. "It's all right." I started toward the hall, then stopped. "Can you get me the file on Ms. Albright's death? I'll go over it with her," I said.

"I can do that," he said, softening his tone.

I shook my head at him and walked away. Sgt. Dennis and I got along most of the time. Mainly because I gave as good as I got, which earned the respect of him and a few of the older officers on our team. Didn't stop us from butting heads, though. Nor did it stop the occasional questioning of my skills.

It was standard procedure for all reported deaths in Silverwood to be looked at by a detective. It was one of the many changes Chief Declouette implemented when she joined our team. Of course, those changes took place under our previous mayor, who was a lot younger and more forward leaning. The recently elected mayor felt old ways worked best and didn't like the way *"A young head-strong black woman was changing things in his town."*

While I couldn't speak to the past, I knew of at least one case in Silverwood being mishandled due to the "old way" of doing things, leading to a perpetrator going free.

I STOPPED AT THE FIRST INTERROGATION ROOM ON the left, next to the stairs that led down to the medical examiner's office. Past the stairs were the town offices, housing all the government agencies. The top floor was reserved for our mayor. I didn't think it was wise to house us all in the same building. If a fire broke out, we'd lose everything. But no one asked my opinion. So I saw no point in giving it.

Before I could step inside and join my partner, Detective Gautier came jogging up to me, manilla file in one hand and a tablet in another. Despite the relenting heat of the south, Gautier always wore a suit. Reminding me of those models in the mens' magazines. Handsome and a year younger than me, he was a recent hire from the Savannah

Police Department and the most meticulous investigator I ever met.

"Dennis gave this to me," he said, thrusting the file toward me.

"He just happened to have it on hand, huh?"

We usually logged all our reports online, but some of the older detectives preferred to still work from paper. Which led to extra work, as we used both methods to keep the peace. I didn't mind, though. Paper files were easier to spread out and look at evidence all at once, instead of constantly swiping from one page to the next and back again.

Gautier chuckled. "Yeah."

I shook my head. "Of course."

Gautier smiled. "He's a little put out by all the womanly hysterics."

"Did he really say that?"

"Yes." He dipped his head toward the door. "You want me to sit in on this one?"

I shrugged. "Couldn't hurt."

We walked into the room and found Raphael sitting quietly across from Odette Palmer. She had a wad of tissue in her hand, eyes cast down as if at any moment she would drop off to sleep.

"Can I get you some coffee?" I asked.

She looked up, red eyes focusing on me. "Yes," she nodded. "I could use the caffeine."

"I'll grab it," Gautier said. "You want anything in it, ma—Ms. Odette."

She gave a dry chuckle. "I got out of hand out there. I don't mind anyone calling me ma'am." Her lips thinned. "But he just rubbed me the wrong damn way. I hate condescending whi—men." She bit off white, but we all heard it.

"I can relate to that," I said, sitting down. "I have to work with him." Dennis wasn't as bad as the others. He was more prone to stubborn pride than outright racism. But I didn't need to clarify that for her. Nor did I need to contradict her feelings.

"That's unfortunate," she said softly.

Raphael nodded, also avoiding any further discussion, and said, "I'm sorry for your loss. We all knew Ms. Albright. She used to go to church with my mother. I've even had her pecan pie on occasion."

Odette gave us a strained smile that looked almost painful. Like she wasn't used to the gesture. "She did love baking." She stared at us, eyes searching. "Thank you," she said finally. Then she cleared her throat and looked away.

Gautier came back into the room with a steaming mug of coffee and set it in front of her. Then he pulled a chair from the table and positioned it near the door.

I took my work phone out and set it on the table. "Do you mind if I record this?"

She stared at the phone for a minute, as if trying to puzzle out the need for the device.

"I prefer this to notes," I said, giving her an answer to her unasked question.

Despite my inclination for the written word, I rarely took notes during an interview. I preferred to observe the person I was talking to. Their body language. Eye contact. Nervous ticks. All these things told a story. Words can be rehearsed. And yes, some movement can as well. But if I kept a person talking long enough, they'd relax, and it was then I'd get the true picture. I'd transcribe the conversation later.

"Tell us why you believe Ms. Albright was murdered," I said.

She pulled in a deep breath, letting it out slowly. "Well now, I've driven all this way and suddenly my story don't make sense to me."

"Why don't you let us be the judge of that?" Raphael offered.

She stared at the table for a while, then said, "I have to explain why I wasn't at her funeral."

"You don't—"

"Yes, I do," she said, cutting me off. "Yes. Yes," she repeated, voice laced with sadness and guilt. She took a sip of her coffee and held the mug in her hands. "A person can take only so much in life before they break. I've spent my entire life with a man who, from day one, lied to me. I lived inside that lie for so long." She looked up suddenly. "Funny thing is, somewhere deep inside of me, I knew he was lying." She finished her coffee and set the mug on the table.

"I've always wanted children. Sorry, I'm gonna have to tell this story my way. I need...need...need someone to understand."

I reached out and touched her cool, dry hand. She flinched, and I pulled away. "I apologize." She just stared at me out of eyes that seemed...empty. Like she'd become a shell of a person. Then, as if she'd been shoved, she grabbed my hand, and her eyes filled with sorrow and pain. This poor woman was searching for someone to just show they cared.

"You tell it how you need to," I said.

She nodded briskly and let go of my hand.

I started to turn off the recorder, then stopped. Maybe she would take a while to get to the reason she was here. But during that time, she might give us a clue as to why she believed Ms. Albright was murdered. I didn't want to miss anything.

"Thank you," she said, not looking at me. "The lie."
Again, she paused, tapping her finger on the envelope as if
she were reminding herself why she was there. "I met my
ex-husband when I was eighteen, at my graduation. All the
local high schools were at a mass ceremony at Bridges Audi-
torium in Claremont, California. He was graduating from
Ganesha and I from Garey." She stopped and a smile
spread across her face. "My friends and I kept sneaking
pictures of him and his friends." She laughed then. "Boy,
was I something else. Fas', they would say here in the
south."

I let out a dry chuckle. "I think we all did some embarrassing things at that age."

She nodded. "Well. He caught me. So, yes. That was
embarrassing." Another pause—this one much longer. "I'll
skip the silly flirting and flash forward a bit. We started
dating. Of course. We talked about dreams and goals and all
those things you do when you're young and your whole life is
ahead of you. All you see are endless possibilities." She looked
at me. "For me. I wanted a family. A career, too, as a journal-
ist. But mostly, a family. Five kids." She smiled wide, eyes
lighting. "It was a lot, and he readily agreed. That should
have been my first sign."

She picked up her empty coffee mug and put it down
again.

"Let me get you some more coffee," Gautier offered.

She shook her head. "No. Better make it water. I plan on
sleeping for a long while after this. Driving all night is for the
young. And I'm not young anymore."

Gautier left the room, and she opened the envelope and
pulled out a worn leather book with remnants of gold
lettering on the front. I could just barely make out a capital *C*

and a lowercase *n*. It was as if someone had defaced the front, removing the title with a sharp blade.

"We tried for years with no success," she continued. "Finally, I suggested we go see a fertility specialist. He didn't like the idea but said he would, but he had to do it on his own. Claimed he would be embarrassed if he learned he was the problem." Her hand curled into a fist. "Another fucking red flag."

Gautier came back into the room and handed out water bottles, then moved back to the corner, watchful. I caught a glimpse of confusion in his eyes when he stared at Odette. When he found me looking at him, he shrugged, and I returned my gaze to Odette.

After almost emptying the bottle of water, she resumed her story. "He swore the doctors said he was fine. And I believed him. By this time, my career was well underway, and I figured maybe it wasn't the right time to start a family. I was traveling on assignments, and he had just gotten a promotion at work, which meant he'd be spending long hours at the office."

Two years before my fortieth birthday, I suggested we might try adoption instead. I'd settled on one child and figured since it was not happening for us, we might as well make a home for a child in need." She smiled. "Like my Aunt Natalie. She loved having foster children since she couldn't have any of her own...well, at least that's what she told us." She stopped suddenly, her gaze on the envelope in front of her. "Seems I'm surrounded by liars."

A quick shake of her head and she continued. "Another flash forward and I'd already started the process and everything was on track. Home visit; background check; health check; income verification, everything. Everything. Done.

Ready to go. And I got a call from the foster agency asking about my application withdrawal." She jerked straight. "Oh, but first," she stabbed at the air. "They gave me condolences on my loss and understood that I didn't want to be contacted but wanted to know why and, despite my husband's wishes, decided to call."

"What loss?" I asked.

She let out a dry, humorless laugh. "The imaginary baby I was pregnant with. Apparently, I'd had so many complications that I just wanted to heal, and now wasn't the right time to adopt. Here I was trying and surprise, surprise, I managed to get pregnant and lose the baby without my ever knowing!"

I watched her as the anger slowly morphed into pain. All the while, we sat there silently, waiting. I was starting to get a picture of what Odette Palmer needed. Of why she wanted to take this route in telling us. Of why she said a person could only take so much. She had been betrayed in the most painful way. There was simply no coming back from that kind of willful cruelty.

"I confronted him that night. At first, he tried to deny it. But his heart wasn't in the lie, so he broke down and...and started crying. He told me he'd had a vasectomy when he was eighteen years old because he couldn't stand having to watch his baby brother and decided he never wanted kids. Here I was, this gullible love-struck idiot pouring my heart out to a cute boy about the future and all the while he knew that future was impossible. But he loved me so much, he didn't want to lose me. Give me a fucking break." She blew out an angry breath.

I glanced at Raphael and Gautier. They stared at her, eyes rounded.

"That fucking bastard," I said. Unprofessional or not, it needed to be said.

"Yeah. He was that. Don't get me wrong, he was the best in every other way. But that lie, it tainted everything. I apologize. I'll get to the point." She reached in her large bag and pulled out a letter-size envelope, then handed it to me. "I tried to adopt after I divorced him, but it was so hard to get my head straight. Then my mother died in July 2020." She dipped her head toward the envelope.

I opened it and found a letter advising her of her mother's death: Undetermined Causes.

"I'm so sorry," I said, and she nodded. "Did they ever find the cause of her death?"

She shook her head. "No. She's never been sick, so I didn't understand how a healthy person could just pass away for no reason." She paused, then wiped a tear from her cheek. "A year earlier my grandmother had died after my grandfather swore she was healthy; they reluctantly performed an autopsy with the same result. Undetermined."

She pulled a folder out of the envelope, smoothed down the package, running her hand along the creases.

"A year after my mother's death, my Aunt Monica died. Same reason I was told." She stared at us. "I started to think maybe I was next. Everyone in our family was dying."

"Why do you believe you're next?" Gautier asked.

She jerked in surprise, then turned to him. "I'm sorry. I forgot you were there." She paused, biting her lip. "I just...a feeling like someone is targeting...someone has a grudge. I don't know. I'm just scared."

She looked at me. "Two months ago, my editor pulled me into his office and told me the paper was looking to rebrand," she said in a rush, as if her biggest concern was getting her story out. "He said he wanted to bring in fresh new perspectives. My whole career had been spent doing just that. I never once stopped growing. But it wasn't my writing. That was the problem. It was my age. And the money I was making. These 'fresh new faces'," she said with air quotes. "Came with a substantial cut in salary. So, I grabbed my stuff and walked out. Didn't shed not one damn tear. Not until I got home, at least."

My Aunt Natalie called me a week after that happened in a strange state. She said the daughter she'd given up had found her, and it was because of her everyone in our family was going to die. She said she knew she was next and wanted me to find Ruby Burkett for her."

She bit her lip, eyes going hard as tears ran freely down her face. "I wasn't kind to my aunt. I said some things I deeply regret. But I was not in the right place. I couldn't take one more thing. So, I hung up on her and two days later, booked myself a flight to Bali. I needed to get away from my life for a while. Didn't even take my cell phone with me."

She pulled her phone from her bag and set it on the table next to the other items. "I returned last Tuesday to find fifty missed calls from family and this package at the post office." She slid the items towards us.

I picked up the letter first. "May I?" I asked.

She nodded, and I unfolded it and read:

Odette,

I forgive you. I know you didn't mean what you said. So, let's pretend you didn't say it and go from there. I'm sorry I wasn't there for you over these past few years. It must have been rough dealing with not only the loss of your mother, my dear sister, but the pain of knowing James was no good.

I never thought I'd have to confess to my own sins, but it seems they have come back to haunt me and mine.

I was fourteen when I gave birth to my baby girl. I won't tell you how she was conceived. Just that it wasn't by choice. When she was born, Mama said it was best she be given to another family to raise because I was not ready for the responsibility. I'm ashamed to say I didn't argue, not because I agreed with her reasoning. In any other circumstance, I would have gladly kept her. No, I didn't want the reminder of what had happened to me around. So I let her go and everyone pretended she never existed.

Seems she found out she was adopted and came searching for us. She contacted me right before your grandma died. I turned her away. And every year someone in our family has died. The day I called you, I got the enclosed message in the mail.

I need your help, Odette. For I fear, I may be next.

Please call me when you return. I love you.

Aunt Natalie

I unfolded the small slip of yellow paper and read:

It started with Ruby Burkett and will end with you.

"Who is Ruby Burkett?" I asked.

She looked at the book. "I have no idea."

I handed Raphael the letter and opened the file Gautier had given me. Her story seemed a bit strange. She hadn't given us a definitive reason how or why she believed her aunt had been murdered. The sequence of deaths in her family had given me pause. That and the letter weren't enough.

I scanned the detective's notes, curiosity piques.

Mrs. Natalie Albright was found in bed, unresponsive, on July 4th of this year. No response to CPR and she was pronounced dead at the scene. I flipped to our medical examiner's entry, Charlie's notes, and stopped.

A chill rushed down my spine. I tapped a scrawled letter in the right-hand corner of the page and Raphael glanced at it. He turned the book toward me, and I swallowed, throat suddenly going dry.

Charlie had a system he'd implemented when he first became our medical examiner. It was his way of communicating with the detectives on the status of their cases without having to go into massive detail until he was ready to do so.

Each report was assigned a letter.

P for pending, usually when he had more work to do on the autopsy but had jot down a few findings for us to work with.

C for completion. Findings were not under dispute and he'd usually tracked us down to go over everything.

He added *F* recently to coincide with the chief's new system of 'Fresh Eyes'. He used this when, despite the findings not being disputed, we brought him something else to test for, he would.

D was for duress. According to Charlie, *D* was mainly for the bureaucrats who refused to approve of a test he wanted to run. Without concrete evidence as to why, sometimes they saw no need to approve the extra expense. Hence, he signed off on the case under duress.

In the corner of Natalie Albright's report was the letter *D*. Which meant Charlie believed there could be more to the woman's death and needed to run an additional test to confirm.

While that alone would have given me pause, it was the image of the family tree in the book Miss Palmer gave me that really got me interested.

The tree looked exactly like the image in my grandmother's journal.

Three

A moment of indecision stole my ability to move forward. My gaze remained on the rendering while the rest of my mind ran through each possible scenario in which this kind of coincidence would take place. It felt like a test. As if someone had conjured a situation in which I had to solve a mystery rooted in my own backyard.

Like the image in my grandmother's journal, the leaves seemed caught in a transition between life and death. In those brambles of thorns and foliage, rested little rectangular boxes with handwritten names scrawled on the sides.

I waited. Sure that the vision I had earlier would overtake me. My pulse quickened and, despite the warmth, a chill ran across the back of my neck. Like spindly fingers tracing the tiny hairs on my hairline.

Someone cleared their throat.

I glanced over at Raphael. He just stared at me with a questioning look in his eyes. I shook my head and looked back at Odette.

"You think this book has something to do with Ms. Albright's death?" I asked, quickly turning from the page depicting the tree.

"Yes," she murmured. "Why else would she have it?"

I stopped and stared at her. "Do you know what it is? What it says?"

She shook her head and turned away.

The book in question looked as if it should have been in a museum. A strange language, etched in gold, flowed down the thick, coarse pages in a layout one would find on ancient scrolls. Tiny symbols rested in the corners of each of the pages.

Most old families used bibles to chart the births and deaths of each of their descendants. However, this book was altogether different. It seemed as if this family's existence had been charted a long time ago. Did my family own a similar book at one point in time? Is that why my grandmother had drawn that tree? If so, what had become of it?

I turned back to the beginning and studied the tree more closely. At the top of the thicket, a single line had been drawn through the names of Sheila and Isiah Pleasant. In their place, someone had hastily scrawled Ruby Burkett for grandmother and a question mark for grandfather.

"Do you understand now?" she asked.

"We're trying," Raphael said. "But I don't understand why you believe your aunt was murdered. Can you give us something more? A murder weapon maybe? Something."

She waved her hand across the items on the table. "This says something, right? These two items alone don't amount to anything. I get that. But together...I'm gonna be honest with you, it didn't convince me either. But I know fear when I hear it. And she was afraid."

There was a pleading note in Odette's voice. As if the guilt of it all was eating her inside out and she needed us to give her some form of absolution.

I reached out and gripped her hand. "Like you said, we can only take so much." I stared at her, hoping she would not only hear the sincerity in my words but see it in my eyes as well.

Hindsight could be a cruel mistress. Giving us a sense of false heroism while we cycled through all the things we wished we could have done. Sometimes it gives us comfort. But more often, it creates an even larger chasm filled with emotional turmoil as we slowly come to grips with our own mortality. We can't save anyone. And knowing that and accepting it can be difficult to bear in the throes of grief. What we had, book aside, was a woman slowly coming to terms with her aunt's death.

Odette pulled away, eyes rounding. "I did tell my sister to check in on her." She gave a humorless chuckle. "I think I tried to convince myself that Oleatha would suddenly care about anyone but herself for once." She stared off—head shaking. "She never wanted anything to do with our family." She glanced up. "We're twins. Like night and day."

"Have you talked to her since you got back?" Raphael asked.

She shook her head. "No. She didn't bother to call me either when Aunt Natalie died. The messages were from her adopted son, Dwayne."

"What about the rest of the family?" I asked.

She let out a long sigh. "I couldn't bring myself to call them."

"Why not?" Gautier asked. "Didn't they wonder why you didn't attend the funeral?"

She shook her head, biting at her bottom lip. "We've had so much death and no one...they don't care. They probably just paid their respect and left. I don't know when the family stopped being there for one another. We visited Mississippi a few times when we were kids, but it was always so cold and distant. She didn't like us being there."

"Some families do drift apart," I said. "But wouldn't they want you to share your concern with them?"

She looked at me. Once again, I was struck by something strange in her eyes. "My aunt would have. We talked throughout the years. She was always trying to help me. But now...now she's gone. I have no one."

We sat there for a moment; I looked at the items on the desk. They told a story. But without me divulging the contents of my grandmother's journal, the story would be a fragmented mess. We had so little to go on. Only a name and a pattern of deaths.

I opened the coroner report again and read out the findings, leaving off Charlie's concerns. I wanted her to provide me with something, anything to focus on, but she remained silent as if waiting for me to connect the dots.

"I'm sorry if it doesn't make sense," she said. "I was so sure there had to be a pattern." She reached for the items on the table.

I looked at my partner, he only watched her as she gathered her things. Gautier's gaze seemed distant as if he were working something out in his head.

"Leave it with us," I said finally. "Are you staying here or going back home?"

"Yes?" she let out a sigh of relief. "Thank you so much. I can't tell you what these means to me." She pushed the items back toward us. "I'm going to stay for a while. Make sure I fulfill her last wish. I wasn't there for her when she needed me. The least I could do is be there now. Find out if this daughter of hers really is the cause of the deaths in my family."

"It's a shame she didn't give you the daughter's name," Raphael said.

"Yeah," she said after a short while. "She seemed more concerned with this Ruby Burkett."

I looked at her. She was holding something back. I could sense the unease now. At first, I believed she needed comfort or, for lack of a better word, absolution from not being there for her aunt. But now I was wondering if maybe she hid what she really knew behind the story of her life. One, I could admit, was fraught with disappointment and pain.

"We'll need to contact the rest of your family."

She picked up her phone. "I can give you contact information for them."

I nodded. "That would be helpful." Why would she have contact information for people she didn't keep in touch with? Seemed odd.

She took a notepad from her purse and wrote down a list of numbers. I watched her for any indication she wanted to say more. But she kept her eyes focused on the task at hand. When she was done, she slid the paper to me.

"Are you staying at your aunt's place?" I asked.

"No," she said, shaking her head. "No. I booked a room at Amina's Bed and Breakfast."

"Good place," Raphael said.

"We're going to take this to our chief and let you know what we find. Do you think your family would talk with us?"

"I don't see why not."

"What about your sister?"

She frowned. "I can't say either way. But I did write down her number."

I looked at the list of her family. They were spread out all over the place. That was rare in black families who stayed in the south, where behaviors were deeply influenced by the past. During the time of Jim Crow, black people found safety in numbers. It was only later, when the laws were abolished, did the Great Migration take place. Which led to millions of Black families moving away from the South. Away from the reminder that they would always be seen as inferior. Turned out, the North wasn't much better.

My aunt and uncle and cousins on my mother's side still reside in New Orleans. It was my mother who chose to move away from the family. Or, rather, my father who encouraged her to do so.

Silverwood housed generations of Black families. The large antebellum homes that once belonged to southern slave owners now belonged to the descendants of the slaves. It was one of the reasons the tourists flocked here. Like the mystery of Roanoke, no one knew what became of the ones who used to live in those mansions. All they knew was at some point in the past, they simply disappeared.

Gautier walked Odette to the door and rejoined us in the lobby just outside the precinct.

"What are your thoughts?" I asked them.

"Seems she had a lot of guilt to unload. But, Bee, I can't say it's much to go on. Even with Charlie's notation on the postmortem report. While I sympathize with her pain and understand it. I doubt the chief would let us look any further than what has already been done."

"I don't know," Gautier said. "There's something there. And something she's not saying. I think checking the facts, asking a few questions, and speaking with Charlie would put my mind at ease."

I opened the book and showed them the drawing of the family tree. "I found this same image not more than an hour ago in my grandma Lucille's journal," I said. "I say there is definitely something here."

"You believe this is similar to the case involving Steven Ray?" Gautier asked.

Steven Ray was a man who'd bargained away his soul to Papa Sin for a reason I never learned. In order to get out of that bargain, he'd used a ritual called The White Birch. Papa Sin himself had given me this clue when Raphael and I'd stopped at Lewis' Catfish and Po Boys after work. He'd told me he was a sinner, then collected his food and left.

Later, I'd found that very incantation in my grandmother, Felicia LaRue's journals. Did our family legacy begin with her?

Gautier had helped solve that case, by deciphering the spell in her journal.

Raphael took the book from me, studying the binding like I had. "This book is old. And I don't mean old as in fifty to sixty years ago. This looks like something from ancient times. I wouldn't know where to begin with figuring this out."

"You think it's important?" Gautier asked, eyeing the book.

"You don't?"

Gautier started to shake his head, then stopped. "It seems...odd. Like the connection to this and what's going on is too thin. Aside from the family tree, what is so significant about it? If it is old, why is her family being targeted now?"

"That's why we need to find someone to translate it," Raphael said carefully.

Something about his reservations regarding the book gave me pause. "You don't think it's important," I said.

He looked at me. "My gut says yes and no." He glanced at the front doors. "She talked about her aunt fearing a daughter she gave away. Yet didn't bother to give her any more details about the girl. Her focus on Ruby Burkett is also a little strange. If she was the real matriarch of this family, she's long gone. So why is finding her so important?" He paused. "I get the impression it's not Ms. Albright who was afraid of her daughter. I think Odette is."

Four

I stood in the hallway, staring at the stairs leading down to the medical examiner's office. "Let's go see Charlie first," I said. We needed to get enough information to present to the chief. Otherwise, she would outright deny our request to investigate.

"Why don't I grab us some lunch?" Gautier said, "Then, after you talk with Charlie, we can figure out a way to narrow the search for Ruby Burkett."

The name had been scrawled on the top of the family tree. Which meant, like Gautier said, she was long deceased. "We're going to have to trace her family backward and start the search there. So—"

"We'll need census records. I can put in the request and pick up sandwiches from Cathy's." He looked at Raphael. "I take it you want your usual?"

Raphael chuckled. "Yeah. And I'll pay. Just make sure Cathy puts extra sauce on that brisket." He handed Gautier a fifty.

"Please bring him an extra pickle, too, so he's not eyeing mine after he swallows his whole."

"You gotta eat faster, Bee. Now let's go bother Charlie."

Gautier headed into the precinct, and we made our way downstairs.

At the bottom step, we were deposited into a dim hallway. Worn gray and black linoleum stretched down the corridor to a set of double doors. The plastic faux windows rattled from the vibration of Prince's "Mountains" being blasted from Charlie's sound system.

Four doors lined the right side of the hallway. One was Charlie's office, but he rarely spent any time in there. The other two belonged to the interns that came and went on a regular basis. The last was the file room.

"Should have grabbed some earplugs," Raphael said as we made our way down the hall.

"Might offend him if we did," I said.

I mentally went over the questions I needed to ask. Some of which I should have asked Odette when we were interviewing her. But she said she and her family weren't that close. So, I doubted she'd have detailed medical records for them.

Of course, I also doubted she wouldn't have been made aware of a life-threatening illness that ran in the family. At least I hoped they would have let her know.

Two things jumped out to me that were worth looking into: the deaths and the connection to my grandmother's journal. The former would have to give us the most clues to justify our continued investigation. The latter would have to be done on my own time. Of course, Raphael and Gautier would help. But any use of our work resources would be scrutinized. We'd have to set up at my place.

Raphael pushed open the doors, and cool, sterile, pungent air rushed out. Charlie looked up from his lunch and narrowed his eyes. "Let's see. Barbara got you all going over cases and you came down here to harass me about something. If it's not in the report, I don't know," he yelled.

"Could you turn down the music?" Raphael yelled.

Charlie's eyes rounded, then he reached out, eyes still on Raphael, and smashed the off button on his portable CD player. "Better? Now, what do you want?"

"Your system Charlie," I said, infusing sweetness in my tone as I waved the report at him.

"What letter?" he asked grudgingly.

"*D*," I told him. "For Natalie Albright."

He jumped up from his stool, the napkin from his lap floated to the floor. "I knew it. I knew it!" He pulled open his private file drawer where he kept the cases he continued to go back to and withdrew a bundle of file folders, all clipped together.

"Come over here," he barked. "Damnit, I knew something wasn't right." He removed the black clip from the folders and spread them out on the polished steel surface, setting a yellow notepad down next to them. His dark brown eyes assessed the manila file folders, each with a different color tab on them.

He glanced at me. "See if you can't figure it out." He moved back to his small desk and picked up his sandwich. "It's all there. Jumps right out at you."

"How did you get all these?" I asked.

"I had to make a lot of calls. This family is all over the damn place. I told the examiners I contacted I was doing a study on families and sudden death. Which was partly true. My initial reason for getting the reports was to see if there was anything I missed. Then, I became more curious as to the why these women were dying. One after the other." He took a large bite of his sandwich, crumbs raining down on his blue scrubs. "But go ahead," he said, wiping his mouth. "Look through them. Tell me what you see." He picked up his glass of, always sweet, tea and took a large drink, eyes on me the entire time.

"I thought it wasn't customary to do autopsies," Raphael said, eyeing the files.

"It's not. Only when the cause of death isn't immediately identifiable does the county allow medical examiners to do a basic autopsy. Mostly to rule out any indications of suspicion. But the exams aren't as detailed as we'd like. And for the elderly, it barely goes past a dissection of the organs and a few drug tests."

"Why didn't you insist on one of us looking into it?" I asked, studying the three autopsy reports.

"I did bring it to Jacobson's attention. He told me he was busy and would investigate if I found anything else of use."

"Jacobson really needs to retire," Raphael said.

"Out with the old and in with the new. Chief Declouette is having a hard time convincing our newly elected mayor that we need people willing to learn new avenues of investigation." He laughed. "She said it just like that, too. But I suspect that little weasel didn't take too kindly to a woman pointing out the obvious," Charlie chuckled, gathered his trash, and tossed it into the small trashcan by his desk. "I also suspect the new mayor's time in office will be coming to an end shortly."

I glanced over at him. "Really? Why do you say that?"

"Not one to gossip, Beatrice." He winked, then dipped his head toward the exam table. "Worry about this for now."

"You gotta give us a hint, Charlie," Raphael pleaded.

"Let's just say he should have never picked up the first stone."

We weren't going to get anything else out of him. But his words piqued my curiosity. The mayor had run a hate-filled campaign and if not for a few well-placed ads on the incumbent mayor's sex life, he wouldn't have won. To say the people in Silverwood had buyers' remorse would be an understatement.

I picked up the notebook and read his notes.

"I was only able to get files on four of the women who died. The rest, I was given only a few details. But it was enough."

Mary Pleasant. age seventy-one, lived in Hazlehurst, Mississippi. I read down each of the things the coroner had ruled out. "Why did she need a notarized letter from her doctor stating she didn't have diabetes, high blood pressure, or heart disease?"

"Because her husband insisted; he didn't take the 'old age' diagnosis. I wouldn't have either. Folks are living well into their nineties now. He also said Mary had never been sick a day in her life. And just recently, she had a checkup with her doctor. But because the mortality rate in our community is so high due to these diseases, the examiner wanted to be sure and rule them out completely." He harrumphed. "I think the absence of them puzzled her more than the sudden death."

"I thought they had to list a cause of death."

Charlie shrugged. "We can't always find the cause of death. Sometimes it just doesn't present itself. In those cases, we hang on to the file." He gave us a weak smile. "Budgets being what they are, we can't always go digging for the answer. If there's no hint of murder, we're told to give the family a diagnosis of natural causes. The thing they don't know is that natural causes are only appropriate if a history of disease or illness is present. Not for the undetermined. Not always."

It reminded me of the chief and her 'fresh eyes' approach to cold cases.

I skimmed the rest of the notes. Odette's mother, Vanessa, was listed next. "We have a letter for her." I handed it to Charlie.

He read over the letter. "Can you ask Odette to have them release the report?"

"We can do that," I said. Vanessa died at the age of fifty-six on July 4, 2020. I handed the notebook to Raphael.

The first file was for Monica. She resided in Chicago, Illinois and had died July 4, 2021. Cause of death, undetermined.

"This must be Odette's aunt," I said aloud. "She was young, too."

"Yes. Just fifty-five," Charlie said. "Now, read the next one."

I looked up to find a gleam of excitement in his eyes. Charlie had found a pattern in these deaths and was waiting for me to see it as well.

The next report was on Leah. She lived in New Orleans and had died on July 4,2022. The cause of death: stress cardiomyopathy.

"What is stress cardiomyopathy?" I asked, my pulse racing.

Charlie got up and walked over to the table. "A heart condition. Although, in this case. The decedent didn't have one. It was the lack of evidence on the body and the abundance of evidence at the scene that led to that diagnosis."

"Evidence at the scene?" I asked.

"Yes. Leah's death is part of an ongoing investigation. She fought with someone. They believe it was the fight and fear that caused the heart attack. But she does fit the pattern." He spread the files out over the table. "I'll save you the trouble of reading the rest. Her twin sister, Erika, died July 4, 2023. Her cause of death is listed as undetermined. She lives...lived in Hawaii with her husband and twelve-year-old twin daughters. She was thirty-nine years old. And then you have Ms. Natalie. Died last month on July 4th." He took the notepad from Raphael and set it on top of the files. "No one can truly say why a person is called home." He paused and looked at us. "For those who believe such things." He jabbed his finger in the file as if trying to emphasize a point.

"Given her advanced years, despite my earlier statement, anyone could look at Mary's death as simply old age. But then"—he pointed at Vanessa's name—"then, same day, same time of year, her daughter dies." He shook his head. "Let's remove those two points for a minute and just focus on the death. Because now, we're starting to see a pattern. What would cause a fifty-six-year-old woman to die suddenly? And like her mother, for an unidentifiable reason." He pulled out the next file. "Now, here's where that pattern really starts to unfold. A year later, her other daughter also passes away." He paused, staring down at the files.

"But no one would know about it," Raphael said. "There isn't a database that tracks deaths ruled as undetermined."

Charlie pointed a finger at him. "That's right. Unless you wander onto one of them conspiracy sites, there isn't a way to connect families causes of deaths. It would rely on the family making those connections and since no one raised any concerns, a request for further toxicology texting or genetic mapping to determine if there was a genetic cause for the deaths wouldn't be warranted."

"But it could still look like an illness the family carried."

"Right, again," Charlie told me. "And if I had only these three to work with. I might have believed that was the case."

"Then Leah's file came in. On the surface, it does make sense. Maybe there was an underlying heart condition that no one found. Left untreated, stress cardiomyopathy can kill you. When you bring in the ongoing investigation into a possible home invasion, she's removed. Until, you add in the date of her death."

"Despite the findings for her, Leah's death did get me to thinking. Coupled with her sister's file, I really started to see the pattern and thought, what if all these women had died the same way? Not some undiagnosed gene mutation in their DNA, but something more heinous." He tapped the date on Natalie's file, now resting on top. "Every one of them died on July 4th. All from undetermined reasons." He paused again, eyes now going distant. "If not for Natalie's son, Dwayne, making that offhand remark about the family all dying, I would have never gone looking for this."

"Shit," Raphael said.

If Charlie was right. We could be dealing with a serial killer. One who had a fixation with Independence Day.

Five

hief Barbara Declouette moved here from Chicago four years ago when the former mayor enticed her to our small town. In her early forties, divorced with one teenage son, she spent a great deal of her time and energy trying to whip our precinct into shape. Of course, she got push back, but it never stopped her determination. I respected her for that. The ease with which she was able to integrate herself into what amounted to an 'old boys' club' that treated outsiders with a fair amount of disdain was admirable.

Despite our town having the largest population of Black folks in this county, the position of chief had always been held by a white man. And before I was promoted, my partner was the only Black man to ever be promoted to detective. Now, we had three Black detectives, Gautier included, and eight of the twenty patrol officers were Black as well. Two of which were women. This change in our precinct was a better representation of our small town. And many folks appreciated that. Myself included.

We walked into Chief Declouette's office and found her scrutinizing the report she held in her hand. She glanced up and dipped her head toward the chairs in front of her desk.

I sat down heavily and looked at Bosco, the chief's dog. He lifted his head from the pillow and stared at us out of soulful brown eyes, tail thumping lightly on his doggy bed.

"I hope you brought him something, too," she said, not looking up. "Otherwise, you're gonna have to share whatever you got that's smellin' good in that bag."

I moved closer to get a look at what kept her attention and spotted the mayor's name written on the front. Charlie's offhand comment floated in my mind.

She closed the file and looked up at us. "Sgt. Dennis has already filled me in. And yes, I've already asked why he didn't hand it off to Detective Jacobson when he became aware there might be an issue. So, let's skip all that and go into what you think we should do and why." There wasn't any impatience in her voice, just a calm reserve knowing we might have stumbled upon something important that one of her own had let slip. And now she was in clean-up mode.

Gautier set a bag of food on her desk. "Figured we'd bring you lunch while we talk about the case," he said. "Raphael paid."

"Thank you, kindly detective." She opened the bag and inhaled. "Shrimp and crab salad with French bread." She pulled out the containers and put them on her desk. "You know, I had my doubts about Cathy setting up a sandwich shop in town." She pulled out the last container, opened it, then set it on the floor for Bosco. "But the woman does have some delicious combinations."

After Gautier distributed our food, she said, "Lay it out for me."

We ran through the entire case while we ate. Saying all of it out loud, it really did seem as if something odd was going on. Charlie believed the women were murdered; I hadn't gotten to that point yet.

When we were done, she leaned back and stared at the copies of the postmortem reports Charlie had given us, along with the book Odette had given us. "Well, now that is interesting."

Something occurred to me. "Charlie didn't tell you about any of this?"

She shook her head. "He wouldn't. He understands the political game I have to play now. The tightrope I need to walk."

I glanced down at her desk, thinking about the file she'd been reading when we walked in and the off-hand comment Charlie made regarding the mayor. "Anything you care to share with us?"

"Not at the moment." She sighed, gazing back at the book. "I've never seen such a morbid family tree before. And what is this language?"

I tensed and my skin flushed. The chief looked at me, gaze narrowing. "You know about this, Detective Monroe?"

I considered lying. But that wouldn't be wise. Besides, the chief had a way of getting the truth out of you.

"I do," I said carefully. "But I'm also not ready to say how just yet." I stared at her, hoping she saw the dilemma in my eyes.

After a short while, she nodded. "I'm here when you're ready." She slid the book toward me. "I'll assume the information you have can't be used to help me convince the mayor to allow for resources to be allocated to investigate this case."

"I don't understand why he's dictating what we can and

cannot investigate in the first place," Raphael said. "It wasn't like that before."

"Politics," she said, then continued, "The extra scrutiny does hinder my ability to do my job, which in turn would also show I'm ineffective at my job."

"Which is the point," I said, anger rising.

She smiled. "Like Roosevelt said, 'Walk softly and carry a big stick'. I like that he's underestimated me. But before I can use said stick, I need to play his game."

"If this were anyone else," Raphael said. "He wouldn't hesitate to allow the case to be reopened. Hell, he would hold a press conference claiming the entire thing was his idea."

"Don't you mean a victim that's not Black?" Gautier said.

We all grunted in agreement.

This was one of the few instances in which I questioned my career choice. I'd always wanted to be a detective. I found the art of discovery fascinating. It was also a way for me to escape the abuse my father put my mother and me through. I would imagine a detective coming to the house and seeing through his lies and my mother's as well. It was also the reason I liked to watch a suspect when I interviewed them. I needed to not only hear what they were saying, but see how they conveyed their message. Or, as my partner Raphael said, learn their tells.

So when I finally became a member of the police force, I'd had a very rude awakening. My acceptance did rely on whether I turned a blind eye to the cruelty visited upon my community. I could say that Silverwood wasn't like the rest of our nation. But I'd be lying. Most of the officers abhorred the behavior of their fellow teammates. They'd, on occasion, call them on their actions. But for us, we were expected to ignore the condescending remarks and jokes and unnecessary verbal harassment. Or even worse still, laugh along with them.

We never did. Instead, we met them in that same place they seemed most comfortable and gave as good as we got. For a few of them, it was enough to shut them up. Others had tried different tactics. The chief had managed to weed out the worst offenders and even found success in changing the community's view of us. But before she could finish the work, we had an election.

"Odette Palmer insisting that her aunt was murdered might garner some leeway. He will try to poke holes. Dismiss all the concerns that Charlie outlined as silly superstition. But the abundance of it all will force his hand. That and the threat of going to the press. He's already being labeled a racist." She paused, then added, "I don't think he cares either way that they do. But we got the numbers, and he's gonna want to hold on to his job."

She picked up the phone. "Charlie," she said after a beat, then put the call on speaker. "I'm going to need you to update the cause of death for Ms. Natalie Albright. Seems you might have been mistaken. I'm thinking it looks more suspicious than undetermined." She paused. "You okay with that?"

"I believe I am, Barbara," he said.

"It's Chief Declouette," she said softly.

We all shared a look. The chief and Charlie, huh?

"Mmm, um, I'll get it to you. Ya'll just make sure you find me something to warrant further toxicology." He hung up.

She shook her head, brown cheeks turning slightly red, then looked at us. "I don't want you working on this here."

She cleared her throat as if sensing the shift in mood in the room.

"I get the feeling this case will stray into those uncomfortable areas the church folk in this town label as evil. It's more ammunition for that bastard upstairs to use, and I don't need that headache right now. I'm too close to getting rid of his ass."

We did have a vocal group of church women in our community that, despite all evidence to the contrary, believed the supernatural elements in our society were the work of the devil. No matter how much good came from some of the remedies used by the practicing Hoodoo community, there was still that small public outcry tainting it.

"We can work from my place," I said.

She nodded. "I'll need verbal reports on the...sensitive topics and written reports on your findings that can go into the case file without any eyebrows being raised."

"Yes, ma'am."

"I'll let Detective Jacobson know that I've given the case to you, and I don't suspect I'll get much push back. Now, what's your starting point?"

"I figure we need to make a list of all the members of the family and question them. Then try to track down information on Ruby Burkett."

"What questions?"

"I don't know. I think I need to see everything laid out first."

"Alright. Now a dose of reality. If we are looking at a serial killer, then at some point, the case will have to be turned over to the FBI. The killer would have crossed state lines. Make sure your case is solid before that."

"Yes, ma'am," we said in unison.

She turned to Raphael. "You still got that friend that works out of Larry's Pool hall?"

Raphael's eyes rounded. "How do you—"

She cut him off. "I know everything, Raphael. Tell him to give me a call." She pulled out the file she'd been reading when we first walked into the office. "I need to confirm a few things."

"Does this have to do with the stick?" he asked, a smirk on his face.

"Get out of my office."

We all got up, gathering the trash and evidence.

"Detective Monroe," she said, looking up. "One of those calls better be to explain what your connection is to this case."

"Yes, ma'am."

We left the office. I was somewhat surprised she hadn't insisted I tell her more about my connection now. Even more surprised, she allowed me to stay on the case in the first place. But I did owe her the truth. Even if my understanding of it was limited.

Six

You're going the wrong way. We were a few miles from the precinct and about ten minutes from my condo and something was worrying me. No. Not worrying. Something urged me to stop and think for a minute.

Was it the destination?

While working from my mother's home would be ideal, it also would be uncomfortable. Too many memories vying for space in my head as I tried to sort through this puzzling case. But that wasn't what had me driving on autopilot with something niggling at my brain.

A wave of energy rolled over me, the world in front of me stuttered—going from light to dark. I blinked and the world around me changed. I stood on the dirt road in darkness. Cool air caressed my skin, sending goosebumps down my flesh. Crickets sang in the distance and whisper of the wind rattled the trees resting in darkness encasing the road. Moonlight spilled along the dirt, illuminating a path toward the crossroads.

Five young girls, wearing all white, stood at that intersection, their backs to me. Long braids traced down their backs.

"Hello," I called to them.

They didn't respond.

I started walking but soon realized I wasn't moving forward. I looked down and discovered I had no shoes and was wearing a tattered white dress. Something similar to what I'd seen in old movies about the south in the 1930s.

How did I get here? Or was I even in this place.

The wind blew, lifting my dress and prickling at my bare legs. "Hello," I called again. This time I look around. Nothing but trees stretched along the dark road. The girls and I were the only ones out here.

I looked back at the girls.

They had moved, just a miniscule and were now facing east as if staring off in the distance. It was eerie how they just stood there.

I took another step but still remained the same distance away from them.

They moved again, now lined up in a row so that I could see their swollen bellies.

Another turn. And this time I did move as if being pulled with an invisible thread that tied me to the girls. They turned fully, facing me now, and I found myself in front of them.

Black holes, where their eyes should be, stared up at me. "You're going the wrong way," they whispered in unison.

I opened my mouth to speak, and a car horn blared.

A blaze of light filled my vision along with the bumper of a car rushing toward me. I slammed on my brakes and barely missed hitting the vehicle.

"You stupid, Bitch!" the driver yelled and sped off.

I heard the screech of tires and glanced in my rearview

mirror. Raphael was out of his truck in an instant, rushing toward my car.

I rolled down the window, letting in a blast of humid air, as my chest heaved up and down.

"What the hell happened, Bee?"

I shook my head, still trying to catch my breath and figure it out myself. What was that?

When I could finally speak, I said, "I think you should pick up some snacks and a whiteboard, too. I don't want anything taped to my walls." My voice sounded strained. Until I understood what had happened, there was no point in scaring my partner.

"Bee?"

I didn't look at him. "I gotta run a quick errand and then I will meet you at my place." I glanced at him; thankful I had shades covering my eyes. "It should take just a few minutes. Long enough for you to buy every unhealthy thing in the store," I said, trying for humor.

It didn't work. He stared at me for a long while, those hazel eyes boring into me. Sweat broke out along my hairline, and I cranked my air-conditioner up. The blast of artificial coolness smacked me in the face, while humid air buffeted my side—creating a vortex of sensations. I shivered and turned the air down a few notches.

Raphael continued to watch me, waiting. Finally, he said, "So, we're going to just ignore the fact that you almost ran into the back of that car?"

I sighed. "No. I just had..." A vision? "Just deep in thought. I'm fine."

Something was niggling at me. But what?

"Do you want Gautier to drive?"

I looked up at him. "No. I'm okay. Promise."

"Well, something is obviously on your mind. Talk to me."

"I keep thinking I'm going about all of this wrong. I believe Odette was holding something back and I think she'd be more...forthcoming if I approach her alone."

"You think us being in the room was a problem? Why?"

"No," I said, trying to get at the reasoning. "Just." I stopped, then shook my head. "Something about her." I shifted in my seat; my whole body was sweating now. "I think she's like me."

"A Champion," Raphael said. "Because of the family tree image?"

"No. It's more than that. And to be sure, it might be better if I approach her alone."

He tilted his head to the side. "Might be right. She had to know her story didn't make much sense. It was strange, but nothing in it amounted to murder." He rapped his knuckles on the roof of the car. "Damn, it's hot out here."

"Then get back in your truck and go," I said.

He shook his head and looked down at me. "You sure you want to go alone, Bee?"

"Yeah. It's probably best."

He stepped away, walking backwards to his truck. "Stay alert."

I nodded and rolled up the window. It wasn't like me to keep something from my partner. We shared everything because the trust between us was strong. Yet, what I experienced couldn't be explained. And I needed more time to process it.

Just who were those girls?

Silverwood had gone through a surge in new homes being erected in the last two years—construction companies flocking to our town, buying up all the old, abandoned homes and replacing them with tract houses. Their fancy, cleverly worded brochures boasted about our influx of tourism and the recently added ghost tour that promised to bring in more revenue. While we did have a tourist season that rivaled New Orleans, it was nowhere near the same. But it didn't stop the people from coming.

Amina's Bed & Breakfast rested between the old and the new. On one side, stately Victorian manors flowed down the street showcasing beautifully kept yards and large cypress trees. On the other side of the family-owned establishment was a row of tract homes, all a few feet apart, with varying front-facing designs. I think they meant to capture the style of the south, using faux aesthetics and cheaply built outlines of shudders and mock porches.

I inwardly cringed at not only the audacity of it, but the ugliness as well.

A small parking lot for the bed and breakfast's guests sat adjacent to Amina's on a recently constructed lot. A few vehicles filled the spaces, but for the most part, the parking area was empty. Asking Odette for the make and model of her vehicle would have given the grieving woman the impression she was a suspect. But not getting it showed a lack of thoroughness on my part, which could account for a portion of my anxiety.

I pushed open my door and inhaled the calming, sweet floral aroma of the White Camellia's lining the broken rock path leading to the front door. Slightly overgrown, lush green grass covered the massive yard. A single fountain, with a cherub in its center, rested inside a circle of colorful rocks.

The stenciled image of a slice of pecan pie took up the bottom half of the wooden sign that read: Amina's Bed & Breakfast.

The bell chimed when I stepped inside the cool, vanilla-scented establishment. A short walk down the narrow hallway deposited me into a large foyer. A large rectangular mahogany counter took up most of the large space. Framed pictures of early Silverwood lined the walls. Two large, plush loveseats sat in front of a bay window with an oval coffee table between them.

"Be with you in a minute, Beatrice." Amina, a Creole woman in her early thirties with wild brown curls and big hazel eyes, stood behind the counter talking to a guest.

I nodded, lifting my hair off my neck and letting the cool air dry the sweat along my hairline. Despite living in Silverwood my entire life, I'd never gotten used to the relentless humidity that created a need for constant showers. And my hair? I'd given up straightening my hair and just decided to let it grow naturally, which meant wearing it in a frizzy mane down my back or, if it had rained, plastered to my head.

After graduating from the academy, for one tiny second, I entertained the idea of moving to Alaska. Just once I had wanted to experience a different kind of weather.

But I probably wouldn't have liked the extreme cold either.

"Beatrice. What brings you by my place?" Amina said.

I turned and smiled at her. "How you doing, Ms. Amina?"

"Beatrice." She shook her head, resting her hands on her generous hips. "I'm not that much older than you. Don't be trying to cast me in the role of elder too soon. I've got quite a few more years before I have to take up that mantle."

"You have a teenage daughter," I said, chuckling.

"I was a teenage mother."

"You right." I looked around. Despite wanting to launch into my questions, in the south, folks took some time for pleasantries. "I see you've made some changes."

"Mmm...yeah. Place needed a little refreshing." Her mouth thinned. "Can't do nothing about those god-awful homes on the other side of me. Can't believe the town council let them westerners build those houses in our neighborhood. What about restoring the homes that were already there? Folks move out this way to buy property that has history. Not some commercial crap they can find out in California."

I laughed. "Speaking of California, I believe you got a guest early today named Odette Palmer?"

She nodded, eyes growing concerned. "Yeah. She checked in around seven this morning. Of course, she called ahead to get that early check-in." She paused. "Can't believe that woman drove all night to get here. And looked all sorts of unwell."

"Is she here now?"

She started shaking her head before she said, "Nah, haven't seen her since I helped her take her bags up to her room. Said she had to be somewhere this morning. Didn't say where."

I thought about that for a minute. I was surprised she hadn't asked where the police department was. "She came to see me," I said. "She's Ms. Albright's niece."

"Oh," she said, "I was so sad to see that good woman pass. She had such a good soul, always taking in those who had no one." She sighed. "Shame her last foster daughter,

Renee, had to go back into the system. My Denise and her had become real good friends."

"Have you been at the desk all day?"

"No. Denise watched it for a while so I could get my shopping done. Around...noon maybe." She stepped away. "Denise! Come down here for a minute."

"Mama, I'm busy!"

Amina looked at me. "Woo, I tell you. Some days. That girls mouth." She walked over to the staircase. "Get. Down Here. Now! I'm not gonna ask you again."

Heavy footfalls pounded the stairs before Denise, the spitting image of her mother, appeared at the bottom step. "You told me to clean out the bathroom. Why I gotta do all the work?"

Amina cocked her head to the side. "Just who the hell do you think you're talking to?"

Denise let out a loud huff of breath. "You said I have to get my work done before I can go to the park. I'm trying," she said, sounding like the world was against her.

"Girl, you work every one of my nerves." She jerked her head toward me. "Detective Monroe is standing there."

"Hi, ma'am."

"Now, she's trying to make me an elder. Hi, Denise. You can call me Beatrice."

She darted a look at her mother. "Okay. Hi, Beatrice."

"I'm looking for one of your guests. Ms. Odette Palmer."

She nodded. "I know who she is. Lady that came in too early, waking me up."

"Denise," her mother warned.

"She did!"

Amina sighed.

"Have you seen her since this morning?" I asked.

She nodded again. "She came back after Mama left, wearing different clothes and didn't say nothing. Just went upstairs, then came back down and ran out."

"What was she wearing?" I asked.

She sighed heavily. "Gray shirt and loose gray pants and white gym shoes."

I looked at Amina. "Is that what she arrived in?"

Amina shook her head. "No, she was wearing some jean shorts and a yellow T-shirt."

That's not what she'd worn to the station, which meant she'd changed clothes at least three times within a few hours. Why?

"Did you try and speak to her?" Amina asked her daughter.

Denise shrugged. "Yeah. But she ignored me," she said. "Can I go now?"

Amina stared at her for a moment, then said, "Go on. Try and fix that attitude while you're up there. Otherwise, you'll be staying home tonight."

Denise let out a dramatic sigh and rushed upstairs.

Amina turned to me. "She gets worse every year. One minute she's sweet as pie. The next she turns into a dang she-devil." She stared at me for a minute. "What's going on Beatrice? Why are you looking for Odette? Is it safe for her to be in my house?"

I didn't know how to answer that question. When it came to Odette Palmer, my gut instincts seemed to be malfunctioning. I was usually pretty good at reading people. But something about this woman seemed off. And the familiarity I'd felt when I first saw her still troubled me.

"I'd say trust your instincts. If she does something that concerns you, call us. But for now...I wouldn't worry too much. We just have a few questions to ask her." I smiled. "It was good to see you." I pointed at the ceiling. "That one will be okay. I think all teenagers go through that same phase. And look at us. We turned out alright."

"Again, I was a teenage mother," she said, giving me a look of reprimand. "And according to my mother, she is just like me." She leaned against the counter. "Lord, help me."

I laughed and started toward the door, then stopped. "Do you collect car details for your guests?"

"Of course," she said, going around the counter. "Let me get hers." She stopped. "That is what you need, right?"

"Yes."

"I don't normally do this, but"—she wrote out the information on a sheet of paper—"you got me a little concerned. My whole world is here." She handed me the slip of paper. "I can't risk her life or mine or my other guests. If whatever this is escalates, you let me know."

I took the paper and slid it into my pocket. "I will."

After thanking her again, I stepped out into the heat and made my way to my car. Once inside, I cranked up the air-conditioner and stared at the little slip of paper, thinking. Odette arrived at the precinct a little after eleven this morning. Yet she'd arrived at Amina's around seven and left almost immediately, supposedly headed to the station. It takes ten minutes at most to get to the precinct, so where had she been for those three and a half hours? And, even more worrisome, where and why had she changed clothes?

I tapped the steering wheel, once again, my mind was whirring. Then I pulled out my phone and tried Odette's number. Voicemail. "Hi, Ms. Palmer. This is Detective Monroe. I wanted to discuss a few things with you. Can you please give me a call back as soon as possible?" I left my number and hung up.

A strange sensation traveled up my spine, the world seemed to tilt for just a second, then righted itself almost immediately. What the hell was going on with me? First a vision now this?

I typed out a quick text to Raphael, giving him her license plate number, then stared at the message before I sent it. What was I hoping to find? She wasn't missing. Not really.

But something wasn't right.

A strange urge to find her came over me, as if my entire being had heard her cry out. There was only one other place in Silverwood she could have gone. One, I wondered why she hadn't opted to stay at in the first place.

Her aunt's house.

I sent the text to Raphael and pulled out onto the street. Hoping I wasn't too late.

Seven

A patrol car was parked in front of Ms. Albright's house. A woman in a sundress and slippers spoke with two officers near the property boundary. She gestured wildly toward the house while the officers stood there listening—each casting quick glances toward the small blue and brown home.

Adrenaline coursed through my system as warning bells rang in my head. During the few seconds it took for me to park and jump out of my car, reality kicked in. Despite the neighbor's agitation, the officers kept their composure. Whatever the reason for them being there, it wasn't an emergency.

I walked over and joined them.

"Detective Monroe," the officer said, acknowledging me. "The neighbor says she saw someone in Ms. Albright's house. We checked the doors and windows. All locked. Called her son Dwayne, and he should be here shortly with a key to the place."

I glanced at the For-Sale sign, swaying on creaky hinges. "Did you get a description?"

"I took a picture of her with my phone," the woman said. "She came from around back." The officer handed me the phone. "Picture's a bit blurry, but you can make her out okay."

"Did you talk to her?" I zoomed in on the image. The image was blurry, but I could still make out Odette wearing all gray with white gym shoes.

"I called to her, but she didn't answer. Just rushed to that car of hers and peeled out of here." She moved closer. "Got a picture of the car, too." She reached over and scrolled to the next picture. A grainy picture of Odette's red Prius was shown on the screen.

"Can you send these to me?" I asked, handing her the phone and giving her my number. I made note of the time. It was no more than ten minutes after she'd left Amina's.

A black truck pulled up and parked behind me. A tall man in his early twenties stepped out of the vehicle and hurried over to us, a look of fear etched all over his handsome face. "I got here as soon as I could."

"How you doing, Dwayne?" the woman asked.

"Fine, ma'am. How are you?"

"Just a little rattled," she said, crossing her arms. "Don't like strangers lurking around your mama's house like that. We are getting all kinds coming into the neighborhood these days. Can't be too careful."

"I appreciate that, ma'am."

She smiled at him.

"Dwayne, good to see you," Officer Clark said. "Everything looks alright from the outside. We just want to take a quick look inside to be sure."

"I can handle it from here. Save you the trouble of calling one of us out if there is something missing." I had to get a look inside that house and figure out why Odette had come here.

They both nodded and left.

I turned to Dwayne. "You've gotten so tall," I said. "It's been some time since I've seen you last."

"Yes, ma'am." He scrunched up his face in confusion. "Can't remember when, though."

I laughed. "That's alright. It was a fundraiser at your church. I brought some kitchen items in. Oh, maybe a few years back."

He smiled, but the look in his eye suggested he still didn't remember.

"Your cousin Odette came into the station this morning. Were you supposed to meet her here?"

He gave me a look of confusion. "I didn't know she was in town."

I pulled out my phone and opened the text from the neighbor. "This is her, right?"

He studied the image. "Yeah." He continued to stare at the picture. "That's Odette, I think. I've only seen pictures of her. But...yeah, that's her."

"Well, I'm trying to get a hold of her. Maybe she left a note inside."

"She wouldn't have a key," Dwayne said, then looked at the house. "So there is no way she could have gotten inside unless she broke in."

I touched his shoulder. "Why don't we go take a look," I said.

He nodded and I followed him up the short walkway to the house.

We stepped onto the porch. A wind chime hung from the arch. Its tinkling brought back memories of my childhood and sitting on the porch with my grandma Lucille, reading her stories while she stared out into the yard with a smile on her face.

"You're selling the house," I said, pushing the memory down. I didn't want to think about my grandma right now. Or dwell on the fact that that memory of her would forever be tainted by what I'd read in her journal.

"Yeah. Mom would approve." He glanced at me. "Renee was the last foster kid to come stay with her. When Mom died, she had to go back into the system. That's no place to be. So, I've started the process of adopting her. I'll need the money to prove I can support her."

"Your mom would be proud."

He chuckled. "She'd also insist I finish school." He paused, gazing over the living room. "She paid for my college, so I didn't have to work." He sighed and turned to me. "I suppose I'll have to drop a few classes, go part time and get a job. But I'll do it. I will do it." He smiled through the tears streaming down his face.

I reached out and squeezed his hand. "Ms. Albright did good by you."

He nodded, wiped his tears, and signaled to the room. "I moved most of the stuff out. The real estate agent lady suggested I leave a few staging items, though."

"It's cool in here," I said, glancing around the small house.

"She suggested I keep it that way for the viewings. So, I just left it on." He switched on the light. "I removed Mom's belongings after the funeral." He paused. "She had so many photo albums and keepsakes," he said and smiled, eyes going distant as if recalling memories. "I can't bring myself to get rid of anything. But I don't know where I'm going to keep it all, either."

I could understand that feeling. My mother had been gone for a few years now, and I still couldn't bring myself to clear out all her stuff. Of course, I can't sell the house either. But that's only because it was in her will for it to remain in the family. Maybe one day I'd have kids to pass it on to. But definitely no time soon.

"Have you heard from her family out of state?"

He shook his head. "They came to the funeral. And to the house for the repast. Grandpa didn't want to stay long. The grief was too much for him. I offered to let them look through her things and pick out something they may want to keep. But they said no, I should keep it."

"She didn't leave a will?"

He shook his head. "Just a signed affidavit that the house should go to me. She also left money for the taxes and some upkeep. But not much."

I thought about the book she'd sent Odette. "Was your Mom religious?"

He shrugged. "She took me to church occasionally, but she wasn't one to quote scripture or anything. I think our going was more about being part of the community. But..." he trailed off. "We should check the house," he said.

My first inclination was to ask him about that last statement he'd cut off. It was obvious he had thought of something important regarding religion but might have been uncomfortable saying it. However, I was treading a fine line here. If I tried to dig any further, he'd want to know why and telling him what Odette was claiming about his mother would only cause him undue stress.

We made our way through the house, slowly. Dwayne kept up a steady conversation about his life with Ms. Albright. The joy in his voice made me smile. She had been great to him. I'd known about her fostering children and later adopting Dwayne, but aside from the few times I'd seen her at church functions, I'd never really gotten the opportunity to get to know her. Not like the rest of the community.

We'd arrived at the last bedroom, and I waited in the hall while Dwayne looked through the drawers. My gut told me Odette had been here, yet we'd found no evidence of it. And if she had, why? Was she looking for more clues to give us? If that were the case, she would have told us. Right?

"Okay, this is...strange," Dwayne said, his voice breaking into my thoughts.

I went over to where he stood in front of a wooden dresser and looked down to find a pile of silk fabric bunched up inside the open drawer. He started to reach inside, and I placed my hand on his arm, stalling him.

"Wait." I didn't have any gloves on me. "Okay. Just to confirm. You don't recognize this fabric?"

He shook his head. "No. I cleaned out all the drawers. They should be empty."

I nodded, thinking. "Are there any plastic bags in the house?" He shook his head, and I continued. "Okay, so. I'm going out to my car for an evidence bag. Look over the house one more time. If you find anything, don't touch it. I will be back in a minute."

Normally, I wouldn't leave evidence in the care of a civilian. It was standard procedure to clear the house and call in the crime scene techs. But without anything being missing, having the techs come out to collect a bunch of fabric wouldn't be worth the expense. Besides, we were told to keep the majority of our activity surrounding Odette's claims secret. Showing even the slightest concern about her entering the house of a family member could lead to more questions and I didn't want to cause a headache for the chief.

I rushed out to my car and grabbed a pair of gloves and a few evidence bags. When I went inside, Dwayne came rushing out of the kitchen. "There are water bottles in the refrigerator."

"You think the realtor could have left those?"

He started to shake his head, then stopped. "I can call and ask."

"Okay, you do that, and I'll collect the fabric."

I went back into the bedroom and put on my gloves. After snapping a few pictures, I pulled the pile of silk fabric out and placed it in the evidence bag.

Dwayne came into the room. "She said she did leave a case of water in the fridge."

"A case?" I asked.

He nodded. "There are only seven in there now. Which means someone has been in the house."

I went over to the window and checked the lock. No one had tampered with it. "Does anyone else in your family have a key to this house?"

"No. Just me."

I stood there, thinking. A few missing water bottles and a pile of fabric was all I had to go on. I studied the swaths of material. "These look like scarfs," I said. "Why would she leave these here?"

"Odette?"

I jumped. I hadn't meant to say that aloud. "Yeah." I stared at him for a minute. "I would like to talk to you about my conversation with your cousin. Would you be up for that? It might be a little upsetting."

He sucked in a breath, shrugged and said, "Sure." Then he walked out of the room.

I joined him in the dining room. He sat in one of the six chairs and rested his hands on the polished table. "I don't understand what's going on," he said. "But I know it has something to do with Odette." He looked over at me. "Do you think she's trying to get the house? Maybe my inheritance?"

I shook my head. This was going to be difficult. "I'm sorry I have to lay all of this on you right now. Given what you're going through. But in order for me to figure out just what your cousin is up to, I have to ask some really difficult questions." I pulled my phone out and set it on the table. "You're not in trouble. I want to start there." I dipped my head toward my phone. "This is the way I gather information when I'm talking to someone. I don't like writing notes."

"Okay," he said carefully.

I paused, still trying to find a delicate way to approach this. Then I pressed record on my dictation app. "Your cousin came to the precinct earlier today and claimed that your mother had been murdered." I observed him for any sign of knowing. He just stared at me, eyes wide.

"Did you hear me?"

His head went up and down, but I doubted he was aware he was nodding.

"Dwayne?"

"Why...why?" He shook his head. "Why the fuck would she say that?"

The curse word caught me off guard.

"Mom said her family was not altogether right. She

claimed she didn't want us to associate with them because they were a bad influence and would cause more harm than good. She never gave us concrete reasons why. Just made sure she kept us from being around them. Never invited them here. Only talked on the phone occasionally. But this...this is cruel. Why would Odette come here saying this?" He spoke in a rush, his voice a harsh whisper, as if he were afraid someone would hear him.

I touched his hand. "I'm sorry. I know this is hard to hear. But I have to ask. The medical examiner said you made a comment about everyone in the family dying."

He wiped his cheek and nodded vigorously. "Yeah. That was something Mom had said when my cousin Erika died last year."

"Did you all attend her funeral?"

"Yeah. Mom went. I'd just started classes. I told her I could go with her, but she didn't want us to."

"Us?"

"Renee and me."

"Did you go to any of the other family funerals?"

"No."

"Okay. Did she tell you what they all died from?"

He looked down at the table. "I asked. She got angry. It was the first time I'd...she looked"—he glanced up suddenly—"scared? I don't know. Maybe...concerned?"

"Did you ask her about it?"

He smiled. "I did. Even pestered her for a while before she told me to let it be. I could tell it bothered her, but she just smiled. *'Let it be, Dwayne. Just let it be.'* Then she went into the kitchen and started baking. That was what she did when she needed to think." He paused. "You asked me about religion."

"Yeah," I said carefully.

"I didn't lie. But I didn't tell you everything." He got up and went into the kitchen. "I need some water. Do you want some?"

"We'll need—"

"I won't touch the bottles. It will have to be iced tap water."

"Okay. Thanks, I could use some."

He filled two glasses with ice and water and brought them back to the table. After he finished half his glass, he continued. "I was thirteen, I think." He stopped, eyes going a little distant. He tilted his head. "Yeah. In May 2019. That was the year I'd gotten into a fight at school. Anyway. It was the fight that...sorry, this is a little weird. Strange." He let out a loud sigh. "Okay. I got in a fight and Mom came to the school. This bully thought because I was a foster kid, I was an easy mark."

"Why would you being a foster kid make you an easy mark?" I asked.

He shook his head. "Who knows? Back then, I'm sure it made sense. Now, it's just stupid. But," he said, grinning. "I proved him wrong."

I laughed.

"Well. Mom came to the school and so did the boy's parents. I can remember sitting there while my mom and his mom got in each other's faces. I'd done some damage, and his mother wanted us to pay for it. She even wanted me to be sent back to the state." He paused again. "Mom wasn't having it. She told her, 'Your son is evil and mine set the balance right.'" He looked at me and it took all of my strength not to react.

"What did she mean?" I asked and took a long sip of

water. Ms. Albright had to be talking about the work of a Champion. But only women could be Champions.

"When we got home, I asked her. She said I must have misheard and told me to write an apology to the kid. Later that night, I went to find her with the intent of showing her the letter I wrote. I found her on her knees with a leather book on the bed in front of her. She didn't hear me. So..." He stopped and just stared at the wall for a few beats. "I... walked over and as I got closer, I could hear her whispering, 'I can't keep the balance' over and over again."

"Did she say anything to you?"

He shook his head. "I set the letter on the bed and left. She didn't mention the letter or anything else. Just continued as if nothing ever happened. She had to have known I'd seen her."

"Did you ever see the book again?" I asked.

"No. Not even when I packed up the house."

"What did it look like?" I asked, finally.

"It looked like a bible. Which is what made me think about religion. Like I said before. We did attend church. She had a King James bible she always took with us. But this book...it looked like it was a bible. But written in a different language. And the paper looked old. Ancient."

"Was there any wording on the front?" I asked, thinking of the defacement on the book Odette gave us.

"Yeah. It read, *The Book of Creation*."

Eight

I called the chief and gave her an update after I left Ms. Albright's house. We both arrived at the same conclusion. We had nothing to go on. Yes, it was clear that Odette had been in the house. However, except for water, she stole nothing, leaving behind a strange pile of silk scarfs

My talk with Dwayne, however, did offer a new avenue for exploration. The way he talked about the relationship between his mother and her family made it obvious they had no close connection. So why had Natalie Albright decided to contact her estranged niece, rather than her own son, about her fears? Why did she send that 'bible' to her niece? I was almost positive it was the book Dwayne had been referring to when he told me about his past. Which meant Ms. Albright either was a Champion or had knowledge of Champions.

Earlier today, something in me screamed I was going in the wrong direction. Then I'd been transported to a scene that still made no sense. At the time, I couldn't figure out if it had to do with the direction I was headed or something else. Now I understood it wasn't the destination that mattered, even though I now had some promising leads to follow. It was what we were investigating.

We should have focused all our energy on Odette Palmer.

IT WAS JUST AFTER SEVEN IN THE EVENING BY THE time I arrived at my condo and parked behind Raphael's truck. My energy reserves had long been spent, but I had to keep going. I got out of the vehicle and inhaled the warm night air. At night, the humidity was a little more tolerable. Still stifling, but without the constant burning rays from the sun to add to the misery.

I retrieved the evidence bag off my seat and headed toward my place, wondering what Odette had been doing in her aunt's house besides changing clothes.

I stopped in the walkway and pulled out my cellphone and tried Odette's number again.

Straight to voicemail. I left another message.

I started to call Amina's but decided against it. My visit had already caused her worry, and I didn't want to add to it. Besides, I'd asked her to call me when Odette returned and I'm sure she would.

The scent of pizza greeted me when I stepped inside my condo. A whiteboard, filled with images and notecards, sat in my living room in the spot where my loveseat used to be. "I see you've rearranged the place," I said, shutting the door. "Please tell me you bought coffee as well."

"Didn't know you were out. But I did get soda," Raphael said. He straddled one of my dining room chairs, arms resting on the back, with a slice of pizza in his hand. "We added the family tree to the board."

I nodded, setting the evidence bag on the table, and went to look at their work. "I want to switch gears," I said, then told them what I'd found out.

"I can't make sense of it," Gautier said. He came and stood next to me. "But it does line up with the phone call I had." He pointed to a notecard with the name Cherie Baptiste. "Odette's aunt, Cherie. Her mother's twin sister. She lives in Mississippi with Odette's grandfather, Elijah. I couldn't get ahold of them." He pointed to another card with the name Patricia Wilson on it. "This is Mary's twin sister. Natalie Albright's aunt. She didn't want to talk about the dead and said it might have been best they weren't here anymore. I asked her why she felt that way and an older man came on the line and told me not to contact his wife again."

He stepped back, and I did the same.

"Can you see it?" he asked.

I gave him a puzzled look. "See what?"

"Study it for a minute and it will come to you." He walked back to the table and picked up his half-eaten slice of pizza. He sounded like Charlie with that giddy pride of ferreting out a puzzle and wanting someone else to do the same.

"It took Raphael a few minutes. I spotted it right away," he said, mouth full.

I snorted, then stared at the board. "They're all women," I said. Laid out like this, it was easy to spot.

Since the deaths started with Mary, I traced the line from there. Gautier laid the board out with Mary on one side and her line of descendants and her twin sister Patricia on the other side with her line.

Isiah and Sheila (Ruby Burkett?)
Mary (deceased)
Patricia (no deaths reported)
Vanessa & Cherie (1964)
Carl (1969) Larry (1970) Michael (1972)
Natalie & Monica (1967)
Vanessa (deceased) twin girls: Odette &
Oleatha
Natalie (deceased)
Foster son - Dwayne &
Daughter- Tamara Wright (missing)
Cherie son Anthony

MONICA TWIN DAUGHTERS LEAH & ERICKA ALL OF them are deceased!

Mary had given birth to a set of twin girls; Vanessa—Odette's mother—and Cherie in 1964. Three years later, she gave birth to Natalie and Monica.

Patricia and her husband had only boys: Carl, 1969; Larry, 1970; and Michael, 1972. No one from this line had died. And her boys all had families of their own. Yet none of them had girls either.

"Cherie didn't have girls."

"Cherie, no. Anthony is her stepson, and she and her husband gained custody of him when his mother passed away. But she had no biological children," Raphael said. "This is my work here." He handed me a notepad with his illegible writing covering the page.

"You know I can't read your handwriting."

He wiped his hands and took the pad from me. "Natalie gave birth to a baby girl when she was fourteen years old.

After tracing the adoption records and locating her, I found an article about her disappearance."

"Disappearance?" I asked.

He pushed his laptop toward me. "Tamara Wright went missing the last week of June in 2019. A week later, Mary died."

"Wait," I said, mind spinning. "Do you think Odette knew about this?"

Raphael shook his head. "I can't say. And since we can't reach her, there's no way to know."

"What about Ruby Burkett?"

"Given the age in which women had children in those times, I started my search from 1930 to 1940. I found three individuals by that name in census records. Two of them I was able to eliminate right away. One stood out. Ruby Deliah Burkett was born on July 4, 1934. Died August 12, 1948."

"There's the connection," I said.

He nodded. "They were killed on her birthday." Gautier continued. "In September 2018, a small paper in Mississippi published an article about her and the injustice of her death. They interviewed Dr. Aduke Oyenuga, the founder of the organization, Shared Pain."

"I've heard of them," I said.

"I called them, but it was after hours, so I had to leave a message." He paused. "For an investigative reporter, it seems Odette would have been able to find out all of this on her own.

"Now, can you tell me what you couldn't tell the chief?" Gautier asked.

"Alright," I put down my bottle of soda and walked into the other room. I'd stored the box of journals in my hall closet under a pile of extra towels. I picked up the heavy box and paused. My decision to show them these didn't come lightly. And even though I knew it was the right thing to do, I still had trouble stomaching the act.

"Fuck it," I said and returned to the living room.

I put the box on the table and pulled out the journals. "A bit of history while you look through these."

"Maybe that's a quirk of humanity," Gautier said. "Telling stories to help with the things that make us uncomfortable." I met his gaze. There was no judgment in it. Just an understanding what I was doing was difficult for me. "I would love to hear your family history. But if you're telling us"—he looked at Raphael—"It's us, right?"

Raphael shook his head. "No. I know the story."

Gautier nodded. "Right. Of course, then in that case. Go ahead...Beatrice."

I smiled at that. "I will, Micah." It was the first time I'd called him by his first name. It shifted something unspoken between us. "Right. You've seen my Grandma Felicia's journal. It was the one with the White Birch spell in it."

"Yes," he said. "Are these like that?"

"Yes and no. Besides being a Champion for Good and Evil, Grandma Felicia was also a conjure woman. Her journals have a lot of her spells and rootwork in them. But some"—I tapped the journal I'd set on the table—"do have similarities to these."

Raphael opened one of the journals and Gautier another and started to read.

"These are...troubling," Gautier said, after a short while. "She was a..."

I sat down. "Manipulator. And that is hard to swallow. But yes, she did some unspeakable things."

"Is that what a Champion does?" he asked. "Manipulate?

And isn't one being called good or evil subjective? Afterall, the idea is a concept. One imposed by society."

"I agree," I said. "We often judge people through these preconceived norms. Which is one of the main struggles I'm having with my role as a Champion." I shook my head. "That word is so...misleading, and old fashioned. It reminds me of something from medieval times where a knight rode out to battle adorned in the village armor."

They both laughed.

"But these beings have to be old, too, Bee," Raphael said.

"Every myth I've ever read refers to there being a battle between the two. So, the question is, how do you balance the two?" Gautier asked.

I thought about it for a minute, mentally recalling all I'd read thus far. "When one is too overpowering and almost snuffing out the other, then I would have to commit an act to counter it."

"So, if good is..."

I convinced him to kill his friend. It was the only way to restore balance.

I shook my head. "I can't deal with that right now," I said, remembering what my grandmother had written. She didn't say why or how Good had overpowered Evil, but the act of convincing someone to murder another could only be viewed as evil. No matter how subjective the concept of it was.

I pushed the thought away and looked down at the pile of journals. "I keep thinking she has more. The ones she would have written when she first started doing the work of a Champion."

"Why?" he asked, looking at me.

"There has to be," I insisted.

He shook his head. "Maybe these are all she had. It wouldn't make sense for her to only keep these and get rid of the rest." He paused. "Think about it. People keep journals to help them deal with pain or to chart their lives or express desires, wants, needs. If you go through the trouble of starting one, it's usually at a moment when you feel you need to."

"When she started losing her mind," I said.

He gave me a sympathetic look. "She could have been fine up until the point she started keeping track."

Raphael set down the journal he was reading. "How did you get so wise on journaling?"

Gautier laughed. "I have four sisters. And I read all their journals."

"Oh, that is so wrong," I said.

He laughed again. "I was a teenage boy, feeling a bit outnumbered. I had to know what the enemy was thinking at all times."

We all laughed. "Are you all close?" I asked.

"Now we are. Back then?" He laughed.

"Well, now," I said, sobering. "What I never told you about is The Sin Exchange." I looked at Raphael. "Best guess? It's a way station at the crossroads of reality. When I first encountered it, I would swear I could see all of history being made. I know that sounds strange, but that's what I saw. Civilizations being born and crumbling to dust. Stars. The montage almost broke my brain." I stopped, recalling the feeling of that onslaught of information.

"Who are Papa Sin and Mama Root?" Gautier asked

"I believe they're personifications of Evil and Good," Raphael said.

I could tell he was trying to understand, and he had no idea how much I appreciated that.

I picked up the book Odette had given us. "Dwayne said he thought this was a bible. The inscription used to read, *The Book of Creation*. I'm wondering who defaced it and why. More important, why would she give it to Odette?"

"You think it has something to do with Champions?" Raphael asked.

I got up and poured myself a glass of wine. After taking a long sip, I said, "Yes, but I also need to explain why." I took them through the vision I'd had earlier.

A look of worry washed over both their faces. "Is there a way to control it?" Raphael asked. "Because Bee. If you're pulled into another one while you're driving..." He left the consequence unsaid.

I shrugged. "I don't feel centered. My gut instincts feel as if they're misfiring. Like I'm off balance. And I keep circling the same things. Not to mention, when I first laid eyes on Odette, I felt an overwhelming sense of familiarity." I paused. "That and the book are not concrete evidence that we're dealing with Champions. But something tells me it is. And for now, misfiring or not, I'm gonna trust my gut on this."

"So, we look into Odette. You think she's lying?"

"No, I think she's withholding something." I thought about it for a minute. "Everything she's done since she left the precinct is odd. It's like she's running and hiding."

"Being secretive," Raphael said.

"Yeah. In the morning, we need to contact all the people in her life. Ex-husband, previous employer, everyone. She's not answering her phone, so we have to dig to find the information. I want to contact her sister Oleatha as well. They aren't close, but maybe she can provide us with some information."

I looked at the board. We had the pieces we just needed to figure out how they fit. "I want to visit the Shared Pain offices rather than call them. That means a trip to Mississippi. So, we can obtain the postmortem report for Mary, visit the family, and stop by the offices."

I looked at Raphael. "Can you focus on Natalie's daughter, Tamara, while we go to Shared Pain?"

"Little put out I can't go on the road trip, but yeah. Might be a good idea to see what's been done to locate the woman."

"No." I thought about it for a minute. Calling would be ideal, but in-person interviews would work better. "If you want answers, you might have to fly out to California to get them. So, a road trip of your own. You can tackle the people in Odette's life and get information on the case."

"I can touch base with the chief and find someone to work on locating Odette," he said and pulled out his phone.

We relayed our plans to the chief and booked an early morning flight for Raphael. Gautier and I would be driving to Mississippi.

"Okay," I said, standing. "We head out first thing. But the most important thing we should focus on is why. Why kill these women? And how does this connect with Ruby Burkett?"

Nine

Restless energy thrummed through me as I sat there in an almost catatonic state, eyes on the board, no longer seeing the words Gautier had written. Every single thought kept cycling through my head. All those jumbled pieces of information with no clarity in sight.

Why were twins being targeted? Killed on the same day that Ruby Burkett had been born. That screamed of vengeance and anger. And a sense of being wronged by a woman who was long dead. What could she have possibly done to spur a decades long hatred to fester and finally be unleased all these years later?

I pushed myself up and walked over to the board. Patricia's line had been spared this vendetta, if it even was one. But she also didn't have any twins. And neither did her children. It seemed almost...strange that she hadn't given birth or at least passed the twin gene down to her offspring. She was a twin herself.

And why didn't she want anything to do with her sister's

side of the family? What had she said to Gautier? Right. It was best they weren't there anymore. Why was it best?

I turned away from the board. I needed to shut off my mind. We had an early start in the morning, and it was best if at least tried to get some rest.

The state of disarray in my condo had my eye twitching. I should have asked them to at least move the furniture back in place. I couldn't deal with both my environment and my mind being in a state of chaos.

"Fuck this," I mumbled and grabbed my keys.

I needed some air. Or I might just go insane.

Stillness captured the night. The air held the moisture from the day's heat. It had showered briefly while we were inside. We were at the tail end of hurricane season, everyone waiting to see if we'd made it another year without flood and devastation.

It was a night like this that had brought a being made of pure vengeance called Storm Raven. She'd delivered a justice no court of law ever could for a woman whose whole life was upended by a savage attack from a man named Sam Guthrie. My role as a Champion hadn't been required for that case. Although, I did investigate the attack.

I pulled into Tilly's Market and parked near the store. At this time of night, most people were already home tucked in bed, but a few would frequent the all-night market. Some, picking up a few items they'd forgotten, others hoping to avoid a crowd. For me, this time of night allowed me to order the chaos in my head. Maybe it was the darkness, the absence of light and noise that helped.

I walked into the cool store. A jingle played over the loudspeaker, filling in the quiet. Its creepy tune seemed fitting for some reason. I wanted to grab a few things for the road, including coffee, since I doubted I'd be getting any sleep. After circling the store, throwing random items in my cart along the way, I decided. There was only one place that held the answers I needed.

The Sin Exchange.

I PARKED AT THE CORNER OF LEGION AND DUNLAP and got out of the car. This was the exact spot I'd been in when I first encountered The Sin Exchange. The street lay deserted at this time of night. Businesses closed for the day, some closed permanently. Streetlights flickered overhead, still in need of repair. I stared at the space between the buildings and waited—hoped, really—that my presence would bring the place that rested at the crossroads of all things into existence. Because that's what it was and what it did when it appeared.

It took a few hours of simply standing there for me to realize I was not going to gain an audience with Papa Sin or with Mama Root. And the next time I did, they would have to give me the key to calling them. They'd also have to give me answers.

After another minute of fruitlessly staring, I went back to my car. A wind blew down the deserted street, its frigid draft pushed at my back and a voice carried in its depths.

Fix the imbalance.

"I'm trying!" I yelled into the night.

No response. I'd reached a dead end.

~

THE PORCH LIGHT AT AMINA'S BED & BREAKFAST cast an eerie glow. Its illumination, amplified in the beads of water on the rich green grass. The parking lot was now full, but Odette's car was nowhere in sight. I stared down at her number on my phone, ready for me to press send. I'd left so many messages already that leaving another one seemed pointless. Her avoidance of us had raised alarms inside of me —had me wondering about her motives. This strange behavior screamed of guilt. Far beyond that of a person grieving for the loss of a family member, or several family members, all of whom we now understood, weren't constant fixtures in her life.

It was close to two in the morning. I needed some sleep. Yet, my mind wouldn't stop trying to fit square pegs into round holes. Nor would it stop obsessing over the notion that yes, there was an imbalance. I felt it the moment I'd laid eyes on Odette Palmer. Something about her was wrong. Or could my niggling concern about her well-being mean something even more sinister was at play here? That she, too, was in danger. She may not have given birth to girls, but her family was being targeted. For whatever reason, their very existence had come under threat.

"Fuck!" I screamed. Why didn't this case make sense?

I started my car, then stopped. Maybe that was the problem. I was trying too hard to make it make sense. There might not be a case at all. No. That's wrong. The three deaths we had autopsy reports for resembled a pattern. Even Charlie picked up on it. A pattern that could indicate a serial killer.

I pulled away from the curb. I'd look for Odette at her

aunt's house, and then call it a night. If I couldn't find her and she didn't respond by morning, I'd report her missing.

My stomach dropped, and I slammed on the brakes. An unseen force shoved me against my seat, pinning me there.

My ears popped, as all sound cut off in a dizzying snap.

The world shifted, as if the earth had been knocked out of orbit. A rush of cold wind slammed against me, biting into my vulnerable skin.

A viselike grip squeezed my head. I opened my mouth to scream, but no sound came out.

I couldn't move.

Panic set in, my eyes darting from one place to the next and finding only dark houses on either side. Adrenaline coursed through my body, heating me from within. Goosebumps broke along my arms as sweat drenched my entire body.

Help me, I screamed in my head.

Every muscle in my body strained as I tried to move. The cold just kept coming, over and over again. My teeth rattled inside my mouth. Tears streamed down my face. I could smell my skin cooking alive.

Darkness.

I blinked and blinked, but still no light shone.

A loud boom shook my core.

A kaleidoscope of images rushed at me.

Worlds, buildings, roads, people: all converged into one space. Flashes of light stabbed my eyes.

A baby cried as it took its first breath.

Then another baby, its cries weaker. Like it was too far away for me to hear.

Darkness claimed my vision again.

"Hello?" I managed to croak out, my voice echoing inside the void.

The scent of ginger laced with decay rushed up my nose and into my mouth. I coughed but couldn't get that cloying taste out. I tried to speak again, but the words came out garbled.

Cool air buffeted my skin, and I still couldn't move.

A pinpoint of light appeared inside the pitch black. The energy from its illumination ran along my skin, further heating me.

It grew. Folding, twisting, forming, until it beat back into the darkness. I couldn't shut my eyes to the light.

My breathing grew shallow.

Then the light split, a jagged scar tearing down the middle. One side blindingly bright. The other eaten by the darkness. Red light shone behind the divided mass.

It reached for me, and I screamed. This time, my voice reverberated.

An inferno of pure heat and fire erupted and raced across every inch of my body.

With every fiber of my being—a will born of pure fear and rage—I shoved with all my might and, with a jolt, dislodged myself from the seat, my body thumped to my living floor.

Hyperventilating, I took in my surroundings. How had I gotten home? I dug my fingers into the carpet, trying to reassure myself I really was in my apartment even if I had no idea how I'd got here. The last time this happened, I came to in the same place I'd been when I'd been transported. Why was this time different?

I stared at my welt-covered arm lying on the floor. I must have really gone to that place.

"How?" I managed before wood splintered and the door burst open. Raphael stepped inside—gun ready. "Bee," he said, eyes wide.

I sucked in a chard breath. "How?" I managed again before darkness claimed me once more.

I JOLTED, COMING TO, AS WATER POUNDED ON MY feverish skin. I was in the tub, wearing my bra and panties. I stared at the red welts that ran along my arms and legs. They reminded me of stretch marks before they became embedded in the skin.

I glanced up and found Raphael standing next to the tub with his phone to his ear. He looked down at me. "Hold on. She's awake." He knelt, coming to eye level and asked, "What happened, Bee?"

I shook my head, easing up, only to slide back down into the slick tub. "Help me up," I said.

He shut off the water and reached for me. I clasped his hand and stood. "What are you doing here?" I asked. It was a dumb question when so many more needed answering. Like what the fuck just happened and how did I get home?

"You called me, remember?"

I shook my head, trying to clear the brain fog. Did I even leave? Had I been here the whole time imagining going to the store and trying to find The Sin Exchange? Dreaming I'd been at Amira's Bed and Breakfast again?

"What did I say?"

"One phrase. 'We are born in sin' over and over. I kept trying to get through to you, but you wouldn't stop saying that." His eyes were a little wild. He touched my head. "Your skin was smoking when I finally got inside the house. Sorry about your door. But the screams."

"I was screaming, too?"

"Yes, like you were on fire." He ran his hand over my arm. "The redness is fading." He shook his head and then stumbled back and rested against the sink. "That was some crazy shit, Bee." He let out a loud sigh and rubbed his forehead with his fingertips like he was trying to ease an ache. "We have to figure out how to control it."

"We?" I asked.

He nodded. "Yeah. We."

I grabbed my towel and dried my face and arms. I needed to order my thoughts. I'd left my house after eleven. Stood on the street staring at the space where The Sin Exchange should have been for hours. Then I'd driven to Amina's. It was two in the morning when I'd arrived there. "What time was it when I called you?" I asked, piecing the night together.

"A little after one. I could hear background noise, but I couldn't make it out."

Around the time, I would have arrived at the corner of Legion and Dunlap. Which meant I had gotten inside. I took him through what I believed had happened.

"Why were you looking for Odette?" he asked, then raised his hand. "I gotta take this shit in order. So, yeah. I acknowledge the fact you were probably pulled into that place, but...I can't deal with that right now."

"I understand. I can't either," I said, letting out a dry chuckle. "I just can't shake the feeling in my gut that something has happened to her. "

"I'll get Sgt. Dennis to send out an APB."

"Did you know your door is wide open?" Someone called out from the other room.

Gautier.

My eyes widened. "You called him?"

"Bee, it's six in the morning. We need to head out by seven so you two can drop me off at the airport."

I stood there; mouth agape. Not only had I managed to get sucked into The Sin Exchange unawares, but I'd also lost time as well.

"Is my car out front?" I asked as Gautier walked into the room.

"Yeah. Parked a little haphazard. But given what you just went through. It's understandable." He looked at Gautier. "Hey, man."

"Hello to you all as well," he said, eyeing me. "It happened again?"

I gave him a half smile. "Yeah."

Raphael touched my arm. "Get dressed. I'll call Andy's and have someone come out to repair your door. I'll get an officer to watch the place until they arrive."

"I can make coffee and bacon sandwiches," Gautier offered.

Raphael put his phone to his ear. "Make me three... hello," he said walking down the hall toward the front room.

Gautier gave me one last look before following him.

When they left, I looked at myself in the mirror. There wasn't a mark on me. But the memory of that fire consuming me remained. I could still feel its heat, as it torched my skin. Still feel the bone chill that seemed to freeze my bones. I didn't understand how those two opposing elements could affect me at the same time. But they had. It was like my body had become a cosmic duality.

We are born in Sin.

Was that what I'd witnessed last night? The birth of Sin?

Ten

A tall black man with rich dark skin and gold glyphs covering his entire body stood in the middle of the road. He wore a long dark coat and a black top hat. His coat lay open to reveal a murky black hole of twisting souls reaching for a way out of the chasm. His head came up and those deep chestnut eyes found mine.

Restore the balance.

Gautier's car bore down on him. But Papa Sin didn't move. He just stood there with a wide smile on his face, while souls writhed and twisted inside his chest cavity.

I lifted my arm slowly, my mouth open, ready to scream, then the car drove through his form, turning him into dust. Only for him to form again a few yards away.

I screamed.

The vehicle swerved, heading toward the ditch in the center of the highway.

Papa Sin rushed toward the car; his mouth stretched wide as if he were going to devour us.

Gautier righted the car, bringing us back into the lane.

"What's wrong?" he demanded.

I became aware of my surroundings before I could fully pull myself from the vision. I was between the state of sleep and wakefulness. And I couldn't find my way out.

The world around me flowed as if a wave of reality had hit it.

Gautier touched my arm, and I surged forward, my chest slamming into the seatbelt. I let out a long sigh, riding out the pain, and swallowed the scream.

I rubbed my tired eyes and looked out of the passenger window into the darkness.

Soft music played on the radio, creating an appreciated calm.

"What happened?" Gautier asked.

"Bad dream," I said, still unsteady.

"Wanna stop?" Gautier asked.

I glanced at him. "What? Why?"

"You've been sleeping for the last seven hours. I figured you might want to stop and use the restroom. Or get something to eat."

I shook my head. I just needed a minute. And maybe some sugar. My hands shook as I searched inside the empty bag next to us. "You ate all the snacks?"

He chuckled. "Yeah. But there's water in the cooler behind the seat."

I stretched, working all the kinks out of my exhausted body, then cracked my neck. Sleeping in the car was never my favorite. Even if I fell asleep in a comfortable position, my body still paid for it. "You need me to drive some?" I asked, retrieving a bottle from the cooler. The cool liquid felt good going down my parched throat.

Had I really seen Papa Sin?

"Not really. We're only a couple of hours from Brookhaven. I called ahead and booked us into the Comfort Inn there." He glanced at me. "They only had one room left with twin beds." He paused. When I didn't say anything, he said, "We can try another hotel and town if you want."

I shook my head. "No. That's fine." I blew out a frustrated breath. "Sorry, I fell asleep on you. I'd..." I trailed off.

My mind was still a little fuzzy about details. I'd taken a shower, ate the bacon sandwich Gautier made, drank a few cups of coffee, then nothing.

I stretched again. Long naps in awkward positions always left me more confused than rested. "Did I talk about last night?"

Gautier took the off ramp and made his way toward the fuel station. "You weren't in any shape to talk. So, we decided to wait until you got some rest."

"I don't remember that."

"That's why we decided to wait. You were running on fumes and everything you were saying didn't make sense."

"Wait. Did Raphael get off okay?"

"I took him to the airport and waited till his plane took off at nine. You insisted on coming but when I went to get you, I found you lying on the bed, asleep. They repaired your door while I was gone. We got on the road after close to noon."

That was a little unnerving. I didn't remember any of this.

"Have you talked to Raphael?" I asked.

"He called a few hours ago to let us know he had landed. He'll go to the medical examiner's office in the morning. But he did talk with Ms. Albright's daughter's ex-wife and he's meeting her later." He parked in front of a pump. "Let me get some gas and replenish the snacks." He glanced at me. "Or we can get some real food."

"Snacks will be good for now," I said, pulling my phone from my pocket. Crap, the battery was low. "Do you know what I did with my charger?"

Gautier turned off the engine and opened his glove box. "I have one in there. Whew. Should I leave the air running?" he asked.

"No. I need to stretch my legs and call Raphael for an update. And see if he can contact Odette's sister tonight. Maybe she's heard from her."

He handed me his phone. "You still worried about her?"

I thought about it for a minute. "Yes and no. I just don't understand why Odette's not responding."

"That is strange behavior, not returning the cops phone calls after she drove across the country to involve them."

We both got out of the car and into the swamp-like heat. I walked around the vehicle, working the stiffness out of my legs, and debated going inside where it was cool. Despite the humidity, I needed some fresh air on my face, so I'd have to tough it out for now. Gautier went inside to pay for our gas, and I walked to the edge of the road.

Thunder boomed in the night, followed by a streak of lightning—illuminating the tall pine trees encasing the highway. A soft, warm breeze blew across my skin, carrying the scent of rain and soil.

I found Raphael's number and dialed.

He picked up on the third ring. "Gautier. How's my girl doing?" he asked, almost screaming into the phone. A sea of voices sounded in the background over an upbeat staccato tune.

"I'm doing okay. Where are you?"

"Bee. Hold on. Another margarita and some more of those chips and guacamole, please. Ha-ha, thank you. Yes, I'm new in town."

"Do you need me to call you back?" I said, cutting him off.

"Yes. Yes. Again, thank you. Sorry about that. I'm back. Where am I. Yes? I'm at a restaurant named Puesto in downtown San Diego. Sheila wanted to meet me here instead of at her apartment. She didn't want to talk about Tamara in front of her new girlfriend. Said it was a sore subject between the two of them."

"That's interesting. I wonder why?"

"It's one of the questions I plan on asking her."

"You think she had something to do with Tamara's disappearance?" I asked. If she had been responsible, then the thin thread leading to Tamara being responsible would break and we'd have to change coarse.

"No. I'm thinking there's some jealousy in there. But it still is a little strange. The woman's been missing for over seven years. How was the ride? Did you tell Gautier what happened to you?"

"I was knocked out the entire way here. Well, we're still two hours out. But the brain fog is bad." I paused a chill settled over me as I stared down the stretch of dark road expecting to see Papa Sin watching me. "I can't shake this, Raphael. I'm all screwed up, and I can't figure out when that happened." That wasn't completely true. This feeling started with The Tree of Life.

"I think... Hold on. Hello. Are you Sheila?" A woman said yes. "Okay. Just a minute. I've already ordered some more chips and guacamole. Bee, let me call you back."

"Okay, really quick, I want you to try and contact

Odette's sister tonight and see if she's heard from her. Maybe even try her ex-husband. Although, I doubt he has talked with her. But it doesn't hurt to try." I glanced back at the car. Gautier stood beside the driver's side, arms resting on the hood, watching me. "I will let you know when we arrive at the hotel."

"Will do. Take care of yourself, Bee."

I smiled and hung up.

As I walked, an attack of vertigo came over me. I stopped until the euphoric feeling of riding on a wave slowly ebbed. I stood there for a moment, heart ramming in my chest. Despite my perception becoming clearer when the wave of dizziness ceased, everything remained...askew. The slow progression of the world tilting finally reached its peak, throwing my perception off balance.

WE RODE IN SILENCE FOR A GOOD WHILE BEFORE Gautier cleared his throat. "You want to tell me what happened back there?" he asked, a little hesitation in his voice.

"This damsel in distress bullshit is really getting old," I said, then took a bite of my candy bar. The sugar was helping. A little at least. The world remained tilting to one side, but I was managing. "Just a little vertigo," I said. "I'm okay now." I glanced at him. The red illumination from the control panels made his fair skin look like a macabre mask.

His gaze met mine. "You wanna try that again? This time, use the truth."

I snorted. "Truthfully, the world seems askew. Like it's tilting to one side."

"Okay. Strange. Should we find a hospital?"

I shook my head and immediately regretted it. "No. This isn't a medical issue. It's supernatural in nature and I haven't yet heard of a hospital being able to fix those types of ailments."

"You know that for sure?"

I just barely stopped myself from nodding. "I'm deducing that," I said, then turned to him. "I've told you that a Champion restores the balance between Good and Evil. And yes, every folkloric tale speaks to there being a battle. Not balance. If I'm diagnosing my *symptoms* correctly, then the moment I met Odette, the balance started to shift. Now, I'm feeling that end result and until I restore it, I will remain in this state."

"How do you fix it?"

"That's what I don't know. This case is different. With Steven Ray it was about his bargain with Papa Sin. For Sam Gutherie, I wasn't needed." I paused. "Actually, that's not true. Mama Root had given me a small amber vial filled with liquid to give to Rosette Baptiste. I learned later it was to repair her womb so she could conceive a child."

She'd told me Storm Raven, a personification of pure vengeance, had upset the balance and only a powerful act of good could restore it.

"What would you call Good and Evil?" I asked. "I've been reading my ancestors' journals trying to find an answer to that question along with how I'm supposed to restore balance when called to do so. But so far…" I lifted my hands and shrugged.

Gautier glanced at me, then turned his gaze back to the road. He sat quietly, and I didn't push. He'd said it before. The idea of it should be subjective.

"If I had to go out on a limb and give a specific answer to that question. I'd say it's chaos in order."

I jerked around in my seat to face him and groaned, closing my eyes against the spinning. "Go on," I said and closed my eyes.

"Why don't you tell me what happened to you while I get my own thoughts in order?"

I sighed and lay my head on the seat. "That's a good idea."

As I relayed the events from my night, I kept my eyes closed to steady myself. I really did hate this damsel crap. My tolerance for pain had always been high. I rarely took medicine for headaches or anything else. Yet I'd been thrown so far off balance, I just couldn't see my way out of it. Why was this time so different?

When I finished talking, I waited for a minute for Gautier to respond. He remained silent. I cracked one eye open and looked at him.

"It wasn't that long ago that society deemed homosexuality as evil," he said, finally. "Black people, women who had sex out of wedlock, all manner of what 'they'"—he made mock quotation marks— "found less desirable was cast into this evil designation." He glanced at me. "I needed to say that first. What you experienced...sounds like birth."

"Shit," I mumbled. "I thought the same thing. But the birth of what? Sin? Evil?"

He grew quiet, once again caught up in, I assume, his own thoughts.

"I can't say for sure, but maybe? You would have to keep digging for similarities between what you experienced and what your ancestors did. They wrote everything down. Now we just need to pull it all apart and analyze the hell out of it."

"We?"

He snorted. "Yeah. We. The three of us have been entangled in this twice now." He glanced at me. "Three times for you and Raphael. Given what happened to you last night, it would seem you have no choice in whether you want to continue this path or not. Which means your work is going to always be impacted. We're a team. So, whatever impacts you will impact us as well."

"Thanks," I said softly. He was right, though. My work was going to be affected. Which meant I would have to learn how to deal with the physical effects of there being an imbalance between Good and Evil. "I could use another set of eyes on all the journals I've found and the books my ancestors left. Not just the ones I showed you last night."

"So," he started, chuckling. "Fresh eyes."

I doubled over and laughed while the world spun around me.

WE ARRIVED AT THE COMFORT INN CLOSE TO TEN at night. After checking in and taking our bags to the room, he left to get us some take out while I took a much-needed shower. I thought about the birth I'd been shown. My gut kept screaming at me to look. Pay attention. The answer is right there. Yet, no matter how many different ways I looked, the reason remained elusive.

When the water turned cold, I got out of the shower and toweled off, mind still sifting through the significance.

The door opened and Gautier called out. "Found burgers and fries."

"I'll be out in a minute," I responded, and quickly dressed in a pair of shorts and a tank top.

I opened the bathroom door and the greasy smell of cheese and onions invaded my senses. I smiled and, after accepting my burger and fries, spent the next few minutes devouring both in blissful silence. Even my inner monologue had quieted allowing me a brief reprieve to enjoy my food.

"You always smile while you eat?" Gautier asked, teasing.

I gathered my trash and took it to the wastebin. "Only when I've been starving for a while." The junk food made a dent in my appetite, but I needed more. And while my equilibrium hadn't quite righted itself, the hunger gnawing at my insides couldn't be ignored. I'd have to deal with the discomfort.

After Gautier finished his own food, he went into the bathroom to take his own shower.

I grabbed my now fully charged phone and texted Raphael. He responded immediately with several pages worth of screenshots. My vision blurred as I tried to read the script off my phone. Enlarging it didn't work, so I called him.

"Hey, Bee!" he yelled over the lively music blaring in the background. "Did you get the documents?"

"I can't read them," I said, raising my voice.

"What?" Pause. "Wait, hold on." The noise in the background grew faint. I heard a door slam and then he said, "Did you get the documents?"

"Where are you?"

"At a bar. The waitress at the restaurant met me here."

Gautier walked out of the bathroom wearing a pair of black sweatpants and a white T-shirt, a cloud of woodsy vanilla-scented steam following him. He raised an eyebrow in question.

I switched my phone to speaker. "Gautier's here. Yes, I got the documents, but I can't read them. Why don't you email them? I can see if the hotel has a printer."

"Okay. I can do that. But let me give you the highlights." He sounded excited. "Natalie Albright's daughter, Tamara, entered her DNA into one of those ancestry websites. Seems she had been looking for her birth mother. She received a letter three weeks later from the Shared Pain organization. Her DNA came back with a match to...Ruby Burkett."

Eleven

We arrived at Copiah County Courthouse a little after eight in the morning. The beige brick building sat in the middle of downtown, between two banks. Gautier pulled into a spot and turned off the car. Heat rose almost immediately.

Gautier glanced over at me. "I take it you're waiting in the car?"

I yawned, then rested my head against the seat. Sleep had not come easily last night. Coupled with the over six hours of a coma-like nap on the way to Mississippi, my mind had kept up a constant montage of everything that had happened since we'd talked with Odette. Like I was trying to sort out something, but there were too many missing pieces for me to get the full picture.

I sighed. "Only one of us needs to go in."

"You want coffee? I'm sure they have some inside." He continued to stare at me. "Tea, even?"

I rocked my head back and forth along the seat. "Not a

good idea. I'm tired but still functional. Add caffeine and I might get another vertigo attack."

While my equilibrium had improved some, there was still a slight feeling of being askew. It reminded me of the time I'd taken a seven-day cruise. For three days after, my body felt as if it were still rocking back and forth. The doctor called my condition Mal de Debarquement Syndrome. A disorder that made one feel as if they were still moving when they weren't.

"Did you take the Dramamine?"

I swiveled my head toward him and found worry lines along his forehead. "Yes. But like I said last night, This is not a physical ailment. And yes, I realize that means coffee shouldn't impact me. But I'm not taking any chances. I'll just have to power through."

"All right," he said slowly, as if he wanted to insist, "I'll be back in a minute." He turned the car back on, cool air rushed out of the vent. "Better leave this on or you'll cook to death."

"Thanks," I murmured.

I turned my attention to the document Raphael had emailed us last night. I'd printed the pages this morning in the hotel business center. According to the letter, a settlement in the wrongful conviction and subsequent death of Ruby Burkett had been reached back in 2018. In May 2019, Shared Pain had sent Tamara Wright a letter informing her she was next of kin to the woman.

It started with Ruby Burkett and will end with you.

What had started?

I pulled my phone from my pocket and entered Ruby's name in the internet search bar, along with details from the letter about the young woman. Two entries were returned that fit the criteria.

Ruby Burkett and Descendants vs Jackson Police Depart-

ment was the first entry on the page. I clicked on it and skimmed the case. The petitioners had claimed that the Jackson Police Department inadequately investigated Ruby Burkett's assault claim against the now-deceased Thorton Buford. It alleged his accusation of attempted manslaughter was false and evidence of prior acts of sexual assault were omitted from the trial.

I read through the rest of it, trying to see if a plausible scenario in which Thorton Buford's family sought revenge made sense to the case. It didn't. Not only were the Buford's not named in the lawsuit, but the family name, up until this point, had been hidden.

The last entry was an article detailing the life of Thorton Buford. His subsequent arrest for fraud against a business associate. He'd been found guilty and sentenced to seven years in federal prison in 1976. Most of the write-up focused on his many financial crimes. Only a brief footnote talked about his abuse of twenty-seven women. He died in 2000 at the age of ninety-two, leaving a sizable fortune to his heirs.

The car door opened, and Gautier slid inside. "Damn that heat," he said, handing me a file. "I don't know how they live in all this humidity."

"It's the same in Silverwood," I said.

"I think it's different," he said and pulled a napkin from the glove box and wiped the sweat from his brow.

"The only mention of Ruby Burkett online with this new information is regarding a payout and her connection to this man." I gave him my phone.

He read over the article. "Okay. What's your line of thinking?"

I smiled at that. He was getting used to my way of puzzling things out. "Shared Pain has taken on many high-profile cases." I paused, thinking it through. "But not all of them. And I'll hazard a guess and say that it's the family of the victims who contact them." I paused; Gautier started nodding. "No one in her family knew who she was. So, who gave them Ruby's name?"

MARY AND ELIJAH TAYLOR LIVED IN A LARGE ONE-story brick house on Dentville road. We'd passed the house a few times before we were able to find the address. A gravel driveway led to the house a few yards back from the road. What seemed like miles of rich green grass surrounded the house and flowed back to a grouping of tall trees in the distance. A porch swing swayed on a wide wooden porch that stretched the length of the home.

We parked near another vehicle under a massive oak tree. Small children played in a kiddie pool near the fence that enclosed the back of the property.

A short black woman in her earlier sixties stepped out onto the porch and watched us get out of the car.

"How ya'll doing today?" I asked, smiling at her.

"We doing alright. How ya'll?"

"Fine. Just fine." I pulled my shield out and showed it to her. "I'm Detective Monroe and this is my partner, Detective Gautier. We're from the Silverwood Police Department in Georgia. And we're looking to have a word with Mr. Elijah Taylor."

"That's my daddy. What's this about?"

We moved closer to the porch. One of the kids broke off from the group and ran toward us.

"That's my grandbaby," she said, smiling.

The little girl stopped next to us and stared. Her big brown eyes filled with curiosity. She glanced at her grandmother then back at us. "Hi," she said hesitantly.

We both smiled and said hello.

"Go on back and play. This grown folks' business."

The little girl smiled, then ran off.

"We were wondering if he had a few minutes to talk to us about his late wife, Mary. Your mother."

"She died some time ago," she said, eyes narrowing. "Why are ya'll coming around about—Natalie. Is this because of Natalie?"

I glanced at the children. They had stopped playing and were now watching us with interest. "Might be better if we talked inside."

She followed my gaze. "Yeah. Ya'll come on in. Jerry, turn that water off. The pool is full already."

"Yes, Grandma."

We followed her into the house and were deposited into a large living room. A man who looked to be in his late eighties sat in a recliner facing the large television mounted to the wall. He turned and looked at us. "Who that, Cherie?"

"This here Detective's Monroe and Gautier. They come to talk to you about Mama."

He flapped his hand in the air. "Ya'll take a seat. Cherie, bring us some of that tea you made."

"Doctor said you gotta watch the sugar, Daddy. I can bring you some water." She looked at us. "Tea okay for ya'll?"

"Yes, ma'am," we both said. "Thank you."

"Mm-hmm," she mumbled and left the room.

"How you doing, Mr. Taylor?" I asked.

"Doing alright. About time someone came around to

talk to me about Mary. That was no natural causes. They did something to her."

"Who, Mr. Taylor?" Gautier asked.

He flapped his hand in the air.

Cherie came back into the room carrying a tray with three glasses of tea and a glass of water. "Daddy," Cherie started as she handed out glasses. "We done been over this. No one did anything to Mama. If they had, you really think I wouldn't have done something about it
?"

He glared up at her. "You don't know nothing. Your mama was never sick. Never. Folks don't just up and die for no reason." He took a sip of his water, face scrunching as if it tasted bad. "I told you to bring me some tea."

"And I told you. Doctor says you need to watch your sugar. You can have one glass a day and you already had that."

He flapped his hand at her and set the glass on the small table next to him.

"Now," she said, settling on the couch opposite us. "What's this about my mama?"

I looked at Gautier and he pulled a notebook out of his pocket. I wasn't going to ask them if I could record our conversation. Not only would it not be polite, but also they weren't witnesses or suspects to a crime. I just needed to understand a few things about their family.

I took a deep breath and took them through an edited version of events thus far. While I hadn't wanted to include Odette's accusations about her aunt being murdered, it had to be said. Because Mr. Taylor also believed something had happened to his wife. In order for anyone to jump to that sort of conclusion, they had to have cause. That's what we needed to find out most of all.

"Odette," Cherie said, shaking her head. "She's had a hard life." Anger flared in her eyes. "I blame my sister, Vanessa, for that. We're twins."

"Like night and day," Mr. Taylor said. "Vanessa was full a spit and vinegar."

"She was evil, Daddy. Just plan evil." She looked at us. "Wouldn't let Mama see her girls when they were growing up. She kept holding them over her head. *'I need this, and you can see your grandbabies,'* or *'I need that, and I'll send them down for the summer.'* She was always promising. Finally, Mama went to see them herself. She cried something terrible when she saw how they were living," Cherie said, her voice breaking. "But murder? We don't have enemies like that." She stopped suddenly. "I can't say for sure about Vanessa. But none of the rest of us had any problems with anyone."

"What do you attribute the deaths to?" I asked carefully.

She bit her top lip. "I don't know. It was strange. So strange, I had everyone get check-ups to make sure we weren't prone to any illness. Hell, Grandma Shiela lived to be a hundred. So, us dying off early must be due to Grandaddy's genes."

Gautier flipped through his notepad. "Would that be Mr. Isiah Pleasant?

Cherie stared at him, eyes filled with concern. "Yeah. What does this have to do with him?"

"Nothing, ma'am. Just wanted to confirm the facts."

"Did Odette tell you about him?" she looked at her father.

"I'm sorry if the question upset you, ma'am," I said. "Due to the nature of the complaint, we just want to confirm all the members of the family."

"If you need to talk to his side," she said, standing. "I can get my address book and give you their information. Not many Pleasants are still around, though. Granddaddy only had one brother."

"No, ma'am. That won't be necessary," Gautier said.

She nodded and sat back down.

"I think somebody did something," Mr. Taylor announced suddenly, voice raised. "My wife, my children. Not right. Not right at all." He started crying. "I can't convince anybody to listen to me."

I got up and kneeled by his chair. "I'm listening, Mr. Elijah." It didn't dawn on me that I might have overstepped. The pain in his plea just pulled at me. I understood the feeling of being lost so well, growing up in a home filled with abuse and no one listening to my own cries for help.

He looked down at me. "I appreciate that. You find 'em. You find the one that took my Mary. She was the only woman I ever loved. And our children. Godsend. No matter what that man told her at the crossroads."

"What man?" I asked, my blood running cold. Of course, I knew what man he was referring to, but I didn't dare say it out loud.

He flapped his hand in the air again.

I looked at Gautier and dipped my head toward my bag. I didn't want to upset him further, but I needed to confirm what I already suspected. Mary had met Papa Sin at the crossroads.

Gautier pulled out the book Odette gave us, still in an evidence bag, and came over and gave it to me. I pulled it out and Mr. Taylor gasped.

"Get that evil book out of my house!" He tried to get to his feet and ended up falling back in the chair. I straightened and, after thrusting the book at Gautier, helped Mr. Elijah right himself.

"What's wrong, Daddy?" Cherie asked, rushing over. "What evil?" She looked at the book. "I don't understand what's going on, but it's upsetting my daddy."

"I'm sorry about that, ma'am. But your sister Natalie sent this book to Odette along with a letter claiming she was going to..." I looked down at Mr. Taylor. His eyes were wild.

"She swore she'd gotten rid of that book. She swore." He let out a sob. "That man told her she'd birth evil. That twins were broken." He caved in on himself, chest heaving as he cried.

"I better take him to his room," Cherie said, her face filled with concern.

Gautier got up and helped her take him in the back. I stood there berating myself for upsetting him. I shouldn't have asked about the book. But I had to get answers, right?

Cherie and Gautier came back into the room. "I'm so sorry," I said.

She gave me a gesture similar to her father's. "He's been getting more agitated lately. Some days are okay. Others—" She shrugged. "Can I look at the book?"

I nodded and handed it to her. She sat on the couch and opened it carefully as if she were afraid of its contents. "This is our family tree," she said in a whisper. She looked at me. "Why would Natalie have this?" She shook her head. "Where did Mama..." She glanced toward the back room as if she were debating going to ask her father. She turned the page, flipping a little quicker now as if she were searching for answers. "This is old. And what is this language?"

"We're still trying to determine that," I said carefully. "Are you sure you don't recognize it? Maybe heard about it?"

She shook her head and shut the book. "I don't know where this book came from or why Natalie gave it to Odette." She handed it back to me.

"You father said it belonged to your mother," Gautier said. "You believe him?"

She just stared at him. As if she didn't want to acknowledge the obvious. We weren't going to get anything else out of them regarding the book.

"Ms. Natalie also said her daughter, Tamara, had found her."

She sucked in a breath. "Oh, dear God." She pulled a wad of tissue from her pocket. "Thank you for not bringing that up in front of Daddy. What happened to my sister still haunts him. Haunts all of us. But him especially." She dabbed at her eyes. "He blames himself for not protecting her. But you'd think the church was a safe place." She frowned. "Look. Natalie, despite how she became pregnant, did not want to give that baby up. She blamed everyone for what happened."

I started to pull Natalie's letter to Odette out, but stopped. Maybe her thoughts on it had changed over the years because, according to the letter, she had wanted to give the baby up.

"Has Tamara contacted anyone else in the family?" I asked.

She shook her head vehemently.

"Have you ever heard the name Ruby Burkett before?"

"No," she said, brows creasing. "I haven't. Is that the woman who adopted Tamara?"

"No," I said. "Do you know who her adoptive parents are?"

She shook her head. "Natalie didn't want to know. It made it easier for her to put it in the past." she said.

We asked her about the rest of her family, mainly her mother's twin sister. But no one had kept in touch with that side of the family. It was odd.

"That man told her she'd birth evil. That twins were broken."

Thinking on his words made me wonder if that side of the family was viewed as evil. Which meant we had another set of suspects to weed out.

Twelve

E verything was becoming clearer. The pieces, however fragmented, concluded with an undeniable truth. The morbid tree I'd found in my grandmother's journal and inside the strange book that belonged to Natalie; the phrase about birth and sin written over and over again; the vision of the pregnant girls at the crossroads; being pulled into The Sin Exchange; and the message Papa Sin had given Mary when he gave her the aforementioned book: this case had to do with the birth of Champions.

"It started with Ruby Burkett," I said when Gautier pulled up to the Shared Pain offices.

"I've been thinking about that, too," he said.

I took him through my theory. Was it too big a leap in judgment?

"I think you're right," Gautier said. "And if you are, that means someone knows about Champions and is trying to eliminate them." He shifted, facing me. "They've only killed those who could have been Champions."

"Or given birth to a potential one?" I looked at the Shared Pain offices.

The building was much smaller than I thought it would be, only occupying a single storefront in a row of others. The sign above the door read, *We share a past and its Pain.* I've never spent too much time thinking about my ancestors' past and the pain they endured. But the knowledge of our constant struggle has always played a part in my life. Some might say we have gotten to a better place, but I don't agree.

We may no longer be enslaved or segregated and subjected to the demeaning Jim Crow laws, but we still experienced racism daily. Whether it was subtle or outright, the hate was always present. Our struggle would always exist.

"I wonder if there will ever be a time when a place like this isn't needed," I said.

"Sadly," Gautier said. "I doubt it."

I glanced at him. "Didn't mean to drag down the mood."

He snorted. "You didn't. I'd be lying if I said this doesn't upset me. I think we all get comfortable in our lives and tend to forget that it wasn't always an option. Silverwood is nowhere near as bad as the last precinct I worked at, but it does have its problems. Thankfully, the chief has sorted the worst of it out."

"I always worry I'm not vocal enough. Or doing enough. But then I'm just one person..." I trailed off. "And we need to focus."

"Yeah. You're right." He shut off the car, and we got out.

A bell chimed when we stepped inside the busy office. Over thirty people occupied the small space, all of them consumed with tasks. A dark-skinned woman in her early twenties, with a phone to her ear, glanced over at us. She smiled, then signaled for us to take a seat in one of the folding chairs in the front room.

We sat and I looked around. Quotes from civil rights leaders and authors covered the white walls. My gaze landed on one from Maya Angelou. A single line from her poem "I know why the Caged Bird Sings" was inscribed beneath a photo of her. '

Again, I was struck by the weight of the two worlds I had to navigate. One dedicated to keeping the balance between Good and Evil. And the other, existing in a world where my very existence was constantly challenged. Where my skin color determined my worth.

I turned away from the poem and watched a woman weave her way toward us. Early fifties, she had an easy smile on her striking face. Dark braids, with just a few strands of gray woven into the black, sat on top of her head in a knot. She wore a pair of denim jeans and a red shirt with the words Shared Pain stenciled on the front.

We got up. "How ya'll doing?" she asked, stopping in front of us.

"Doing just fine," I said. "Are you Dr. Aduke Oyenuga?"

"I am, officer? Detective?"

I laughed. "Is it that obvious?"

She smiled. "I wouldn't be good at what I do if I wasn't able to read people. It's in the way you carry yourself. Not arrogance like some, but definitely a sense of authority. It radiates off you." She looked at Gautier. "Yours is easy going. But it's still there. What brings you here?"

"We wanted to ask about this," I said, handing her the letter. "And if possible, I need to understand how you go about finding your cases."

She read over the letter. "Yes. I believe I can help you with this." She looked up and met my gaze. "This isn't a challenge on the legitimacy of the claim," she said. "So, what is your concern with this?"

"We're trying to find out more about Ruby Burkett and locate the woman you sent that to."

She nodded. "Good. Because we still have her money in trust." She turned. "Follow me."

We made our way to the back of the office and followed Dr. Aduke Oyenuga into a small room that held a single desk, a filing cabinet, and chairs. She sat behind the desk and signaled to the two metal chairs in front of it. "Please, take a seat."

We sat.

"Can I get you something to drink?"

"No ma'am," I said. "But thank you."

She nodded, set the letter on the desk and opened her laptop. I pulled my phone out with the intention of asking to record the interview. Gautier touched my hand and when I looked over, he gave me a miniscule shake of his head.

I had to trust he would take good notes once again.

"We're reaching the cut off point for this payout," Dr. Oyenuga said. "The Anthony Lewis Act of 1939, signed into law by former President Obama in 2012, only allows ten years for relatives to be located and paid when a settlement is reached. Which is why we mostly deal with cases brought to us by descendants of the wronged. In this case," she looked at her computer screen. "We became aware of Ruby Burkett through a third party. A woman named Doris Quinn contacted us in April 2017. She claimed she lived with Ruby in a communal Big House in 1948. The same year Ruby was tried and convicted of the attempted murder of her employer, Thorton Buford."

"Did Mrs. Quinn call your office?" I asked.

"No. She came here with her grandson."

"How did you obtain Ruby's DNA?"

"Doris Quinn brought in a brown bag of Ruby's things that she had kept after the young girl was executed. Along with an obituary for her."

"Executed? For manslaughter?" Gautier asked.

She shook her head. "She was sentenced to five years in prison. She was found dead in her cell a few months after her conviction. I say executed because that is exactly what they did."

We all shared a silence laced with anger.

"We used a hairbrush to obtain DNA for Ruby. Intact hair follicles can hold enough material to collect DNA and can last decades."

"Sixty-nine years," I said. "That has to be a record."

"It is." She paused. "Do you remember Medger Evers?"

We both nodded.

"Medgar Evers was exhumed thirty years after he had been buried. His body intact and in good enough condition for an autopsy to be performed, so the man who killed him could finally be brought to justice. I believe in miracles. I also believe the souls of the wronged hold on long enough to right the wrongs against them. Ruby Burkett's DNA should have been degraded. But in this case, it was almost as if she had been waiting. A piece of her, intact, until just the moment."

A chill ran down my arms.

"We found Tamara Wright using that DNA. She had

uploaded her DNA profile to an ancestry website in search of her birth parents." She stared at the contents on the screen, her finger working the mouse wheel as she scrolled. "We contacted her in May 2019. She told us she'd come to our offices and asked if we could help her find her mother as well. She was informed that we hadn't been able to locate anyone else and unless someone came forward, it would be difficult to do so since the case was brought to us by an unrelated third party."

"If I recall, the law requires you to publish the settlement."

She nodded. "We did. And got many calls claiming to be Ruby's family. DNA, of course, ruled them out."

Ruby's real family had no idea who she was. So, of course, they wouldn't have been able to find anyone.

"Did you try to reach Tamara after the initial phone call?" I asked.

"Yes, when she didn't show up. I tried calling again. The calls kept going to voicemail." She looked at her screen. "The last attempt was right after July 4th of that same year. That time I got a message the phone had been disconnected."

Right after Mary, Elijah's wife, had died. "How did she seem when you talked with her that first time?"

She sat back, thinking. "I'd say elated but also a bit desperate. Like she was looking for something more. I don't think the money was her main concern. She was more interested in finding her family. She called them her real family."

"Have you talked with Doris Quinn?" Gautier asked.

"Funny you should ask that. Last week, she called and gave me her new address. She said she went home to the Big House and that's where she'll stay until it's her time."

"Is that what she said? Word for word?" I asked.

She nodded. "Yeah. I thought it was a little strange. That's why it stuck with me."

"Where is the Big House?" I asked.

"Not too far from here." She wrote the address down and handed it to us. "If you find Tamara or anyone else related to Ruby, will you let them know about the settlement? It will be returned to the city in 2028." She shook her head. "That's the one aspect of that law I truly hate. But it was a compromise to get the votes for it to pass. As far as I'm concerned, if we are unable to locate family, that money should go to the community."

I looked at Gautier. "We have information on the family. However, they don't know they are related to Ruby. So, you might want to tread lightly." Gautier handed her a slip of paper with a list the family members we'd been tracing.

Dr. Oyenuga smiled. "Thank you. This is so helpful." We all got up. "If you do find Tamara. I'd like to make sure she is included in the distribution."

"We will let you know," I said, then paused. "Do you still have Ruby's belongings?"

She shook her head. "The clothing was beyond salvageable, but we do have the obituary." She got up and opened the file cabinet. After searching through it, she pulled out a worn piece of newspaper. "Here."

I studied the image of the young girl on the page. I scanned the page, reading the few memories people shared of her. An only child, parents deceased, she'd died at the tender age of fourteen. Right after giving birth...twins.

She walked us to the door, and we stepped outside, once again, into the heat. I looked back at the building. Was I doing enough? I pulled a card from my pocket and before I could walk back inside, Gautier handed me one of his as well.

Dr. Oyenuga stood just inside the door, watching me. I gave her our cards and she gave me a nod of thanks. I didn't know what to say, but the look on her face suggested I didn't need to say anything. After a brief pause, I left.

Thirteen

∽

T he Big House, now named Pleasant Assisted
Living, reminded me of southern gothic images
from the past. No more than seventeen hundred
square feet, the wood structure, with its white paint and dark
green trim, seemed to stand out in a neighborhood now
occupied with modern homes. Residents sat at small tables in
front of the place, while men and women in white uniforms
moved among them, distributing food and drinks.

We parked on the street and made our way to the front
door. An affixed sign just above the doorbell advised visitors
to ring the bell. We did and waited for someone to answer.

A young lady opened the door. "Afternoon," she said.
"Who ya'll here to see?"

I smiled. "Afternoon. My name's Detective Monroe and
this is my partner, Detective Gautier. We're looking for a Ms.
Doris Quinn."

She smiled. "Yes, detective. She's here. I can take you to
see her."

We stepped inside and she closed the door.

"If you don't mind me saying," Gautier started. "You don't seem too surprised to see us."

She chuckled. "Ms. Quinn knew you were coming." She looked at us, "She has what some call the sight. Said you'd be here sometime today."

We stopped walking. "What do you mean?" I asked.

"Don't tell me ya'll don't believe in the sight." She shook her head. "Folks around here have seen all manner of the strange." She looked around. "Ms. Quinn told us this was where she grew up. Said this was the place she was supposed to die." She leaned in. "Dr. Moore has something to say about that. Told Mr. Quinn she wasn't going nowhere long as he was around." She laughed. "He doesn't understand. You know when it's your time."

"But how did she know we were coming?"

"She just knew. Follow me. Don't want to keep her waiting."

Gautier and I exchanged a look before following the young woman down a short hallway and into an enclosed patio at the back of the house. A woman in her late eighties sat in a recliner staring out the glass doors leading to the backyard. Her long gray hair reached her small shoulders. She had a green and white crocheted blanket over her lap and held a picture frame in her arthritic hands. She turned and looked at us out of pale gray eyes.

"Thank you, Rose. Can you bring me and my guests some of that lemonade and sponge cake cook made? We gonna sit and talk for a while. Better get ahold of my grandson. Let him know to come on down."

"Ms. Doris," Rose said, eyes filling with tears. "Now?"

"Go on, Rose. Let us talk in peace."

Rose wiped her tears and rushed away. I stood there in a

well of confusion. Unable to speak. How did one function knowing the exact moment they were going to die?

Gautier touched my arm, breaking the spell. He jerked his head toward the woman and guided me to one of the two chairs situated next to her.

She smiled at me. "You seem a little shocked."

"I'm sorry ma'am. I'm not used to...this."

She studied me for a minute. "I think you used to a lot. Sit down. Ask your questions."

"You're not about to die," Gautier said, gaze fixed on her.

She tittered. "Yes, young man. I've lived a long enough life. Left my mark on this world, and now it's time." She ran her hand down the glass on the picture frame. "Just have one more thing to do."

"How do you know?" I asked, finding my voice.

She settled back against the chair. "My mama gave me the sight. It hasn't always done me good. There's danger in the knowing." She showed us the picture. "This here is the Big House when colored folk had little rights to own anything. Isaiah Pleasant and his wife, Sheila, owned it back then. Took in anyone that needed a place. Including me and my mama." She pointed to a small girl standing next to a beautiful light-skinned black woman with short black hair. "That there is me and my mama." She smiled. "She was beautiful."

"She was," Gautier said.

"Mama was killed when I was seventeen. She read cards for the white ladies at their social parties. Husbands didn't like that." She shook her head, eyes distant. "They found her in a ditch not too far from here." Her hands shook. She pulled a handkerchief from her pocket and wiped her eyes. "Sheila, let me stay until I was nineteen."

"Did they ever find the people who killed your mama?" I asked.

She smiled through her tears. "Isiah and his friends got Mama her justice." She looked at me. "It's too late to arrest ole' Isiah now." She chuckled.

"I wouldn't," I said. "How did you know we were police officers?"

"Same way I know you're here about Ruby." She pointed to another young woman standing next to four other girls. All of them were pregnant. "This is Ruby and the girls she arrived at the Big House with."

Rose returned with a tray of lemonade and plates of cake on them. "I called your grandson. He said to tell you to stop foolin' around and he will see you on Sunday."

Doris shook her head. "That boy."

"He doesn't believe in your gifts?" I asked, handing her a glass of lemonade.

"He doesn't want to believe. He'll be here. But it will be too late." She drank some of her lemonade, then handed me the glass. I set it on the table beside her.

"Dr. Oyenuga said you gave her Ruby's things. Why did you hold on to them so long?"

"Wasn't time. Evil hadn't accepted its fate just yet. But it was getting prepared. Clarity is not always apparent. Sometimes I get the dates all messed up. But your coming here? That I knew for sure."

"What evil?" I asked.

She looked at me. "The evil Ruby brought into this world."

My blood ran cold. Papa Sin had told Mary she would give birth to evil. That twins were broken.

"I don't understand," I said. "I..."

"You know more than you're willing to accept. Don't fight your gift. I did that in the beginning. It got me nowhere. I was so scared after Mama died. So scared. I missed so many opportunities to do the right thing. I won't make that mistake now." She looked at the picture again.

"When these girls arrived. I sensed something about them. Mama didn't want me to be around them. She sensed something, too. They were different."

"Different how?" I asked.

She stared at me. "In the same way you are. But it wasn't the girls. It was the babies they carried in their wombs." She paused and reached for her lemonade. After taking another drink, she continued. "In those days, midwives delivered the babies in our community. We had one...her name was Fannie? Yes, Fannie. Ms. Sheila had sent for her to look over the girls, make sure they were alright. Before Fannie arrived, he did."

"Who?" Gautier asked, his voice filled with awe.

"A tall man wearing a top hat and cloak. He called himself Papa Sin." She stared out at the yard, as if remembering. "He told Isiah and Sheila that the only one who could look after the girls was Mama Root and she would know when it was their time to deliver."

My heart pounded in my chest. Both Gautier and Ms. Doris stared at me as I surged to my feet and began pacing the small space. "I..." The world tilted, and I went to my knees. Gautier rushed over.

"Beatrice," he said.

"Give me a minute," I responded, holding up my hand. Awareness of all the strange things in this world had never been an issue for me. Not until I became a part of that strangeness. I struggled with the knowledge of my abilities.

And although my endless search for answers had led me here, where I wanted to be, I was still having a hard time. "They were carrying his child," I said, staring at the ground. "Champions came from him."

"Now you understand," Ms. Doris said. "They come from him and are brought into this world by her."

I looked at her. "You know about Champions?"

She nodded. "I was there when they all were born. Screaming at the world. The woman, Mama Root, had this sense of all things right about her. Her spirit called to me. I could swear she spoke inside my head."

I got up and sat back down. After finishing my lemonade, I said, "What did she say?"

"Balance. Just that one word." She paused again. "When it was Ruby's turn to give birth, something strange happened. Her first baby came out screaming and Mama Root's face changed. She looked...sad. A few minutes later, the next baby came out. And everything went silent. She looked up at Papa Sin, tears streaming down her face, and said, 'They are broken.'"

"You were in the room?" I asked.

"I hid in the closet. And watched the entire thing through a crack in the door. Papa Sin picked up the silent baby and started to walk away. But Ruby screamed at him to give her back. He hesitated for only a second. Then said something I didn't understand before reluctantly handing her the baby back."

"Was he whispering?" Gautier asked.

"No. It was a different language." She sighed. "I don't know which of those babies is responsible for what is happening now. But one of them is. And it all started with Ruby Burkett."

It started with Ruby Burkett and will end with you.

She started coughing and I handed her the glass of lemonade. "Did you see him...Papa Sin or Mama Root again?" I asked.

She finished her drink and lay back in the chair, cradling the glass to her chest. "Once. It was right after Ruby had been killed. Papa came back to take the twins. But Ms. Sheila was determined to raise them girls. Told him she could look after them. Raise them up right." She looked at me. "I didn't see either one of them again after that. Then, the other four girls all left. Men came and collected em. Like they'd been promised..." she started coughing again.

"Do you need more water, ma'am? Or the doctor?"

She rocked her head back and forth. "I've done all I can do." She ran her hand down the glass on the picture frame. "It's time for me to rest."

We didn't want to push her any further. After thanking her for her time, we both got up and started toward the front of the house, leaving Doris to wait for her grandson. A woman met us in the hall.

"Can I help ya'll?" she asked.

"We were just in with Ms. Doris," Gautier said.

"Ms. Doris? I'm sorry, Ms. Doris passed last week."

We rushed back in the room and found it empty. The photograph she'd shown us was resting on the little glass table. I picked it up and stared at the image, just now noticing the young woman standing near Doris.

The same young woman who'd greeted us at the door when we first arrived.

Fourteen

We drove for a while in silence. Each of us consumed with our own thoughts. This time, I hadn't been transported to another place. This time, Gautier had been with me. Talking to a woman who'd been dead for a week.

"I'm trying to wrap my head around what just happened," I said, finally.

Gautier nodded. "We can spend some time going back and forth about it not being possible for us to have had a conversation with a ghost. Or, we can accept the reality and move on."

"We also drank lemonade and ate sponge cake provided by another ghost."

He nodded again. "We might need to start journaling."

I laughed despite the seriousness of the situation. But he was right. We could either dwell on the impossible or use what we learned to move forward and dwell later.

There wasn't any doubt now that someone was killing

Ruby Burkett's descendants. And the one person who came to mind was Tamara.

"You want to talk about what we've learned?" Gautier asked.

"Yes. If you want me to help drive, I can."

"Are you steady?" He shook his head. "Never mind. You don't have control of your visions so, I'll drive. We can get our things from the hotel, and you can talk me through what you're thinking."

I took him through my theory. All of this started in 2019. First Tamara becomes aware of her family. She reaches out to Shared Pain not to collect the money, but to find the rest of her family. Then she goes missing. Or leaves. Next, Dwayne finds his mother with the *Book of Creation* in May of 2019. After finding her with that book, the deaths begin. All carried out a year apart on Ruby Burkett's birthday.

"It started with Ruby Burkett and ends with you," Gautier said. "You think she's killing her family because she was abandoned?"

"No. It has something to do with the birth of Champions. She wasn't a twin. So maybe she became aware of Champions or was a Champion herself and knew that twins had the potential for evil."

"That's a stretch Beatrice," he said.

"It's the only plausible explanation. Otherwise, why start in 2019? If it was another member of the family, why wait till then?"

AFTER CHECKING OUT OF THE HOTEL, I CALLED THE

chief to see if they had been able to get hold of Odette. They hadn't. I couldn't shake the feeling that she was in danger.

"I think Ms. Albright knew," I said after a while.

"Knew her daughter was responsible for the deaths in her family?"

I nodded. "Yeah. I can't get past these conflicting accounts of her feelings towards her daughter. Cherie said she was mad at the family for making her give up the baby. Yet, the letter she wrote Odette implied she was okay with it. Then there's the focus on Ruby in Natalie's writing. She implied her daughter was responsible, but it's also like a mother protecting her child, even though she knows something is wrong."

"Like Ruby not letting Papa Sin take her baby."

"Right."

My phone rang, and I pulled it from my pocket. "I was just getting ready to call you," I told Raphael, putting him on speaker. "Wanna go first?"

"Okay," he said hesitantly. "You sound a little over-charged. You sure you don't want to go first?"

Gautier laughed.

"First. I was able to get the postmortem report on Odette's mother, Vanessa. It's like all the others. Next, I went to the paper Odette worked for. Outfit called Sun Crest Tribune." He paused. "I get why you wanted to go to Missis-sippi. You might find answers about yourself. But I wish you had been here for my talk with her old coworkers."

"Why is that?"

"It was like they were towing the line between being honest and keeping company secrets. She wasn't loved. Not hated. But not well liked either. But I get the impression that it had more to do with why she was asked to leave."

"So they weren't bringing in new voices?" I asked.

"Yes. And no. When I asked about that pointedly, it was almost as if they were relieved for an excuse and agreed, too enthusiastically for my taste. Plus, the guard on duty mentioned NDA's being signed."

"Why the hell would someone leaving cause the company to require NDAs?" Gautier asked.

"I couldn't get any more out of him. I did, however, get a contact number for her sister Oleatha, who lives in Bakersfield. I left her a message to call me."

I thought about this new information. Why would Odette lie? More importantly, what could she have done?

"Anything else?" I asked.

"Yeah. Something strange. As I was leaving, one of the junior reporters came out and started flirting with me. It was strange because she was so obvious about it. A bit over the top. Then, she asked for my number or my email. It was the email that threw me."

"Did you give it to her?"

"No. I gave her yours. And she didn't even bat an eye. Just rushed back into the office."

"That is strange. What about the ex-husband?"

"I couldn't find anything on him." He paused. "I was able to talk to the detective who looked into Tamara's disappearance. The investigation was routine. They talked with a few friends and her adoptive parents and family. Even flagged her credit cards and cellphone. But nothing. No one has touched the case since 2020."

Missing persons casing were hard. And unless there was an influx of leads, the case could go cold quickly.

"I'm heading to the airport now. I should be in Savannah this evening. Ya'll staying out there longer?"

"No. We're heading home now." I took him through what we'd learned and my concern for Odette.

"Shit. A ghost. Well, that's a new one for me," he said. "You wanna talk about your connection to Papa Sin?"

"No. Let's focus on finding Odette and Oleatha. I think Cherie is safe."

"Did you inform the chief?"

"She still has someone looking for Odette. We should be in Silverwood in a little over five hours. We can pick you up."

We hung up and rode in silence for a while. I couldn't fit this new information into my theory. I knew something had been off about Odette's story, but I believed it had more to do with the book she gave us than why she'd left her career at the newspaper. Why would she lie about her job?

"You still think Odette's in danger?" Gautier asked.

Did I? "Yeah. I think she is. But I just can't figure this woman out. Why go silent after talking with us? It just doesn't make sense. And leaving scarfs in her aunt's house. Changing clothes three times."

"Sounds like someone who is running," he said.

"Hiding. That's exactly what it sounds like. Someone who doesn't want to be found."

"Think she knows Tamara is after her?"

"I do. I think she knew all along."

The question was why hadn't she told us this in the first place? And where was her sister?

WE WERE AN HOUR FROM SAVANNAH WHEN MY phone rang again. "It's the chief," I said, heart sinking. "Chief," I said, putting the phone on speaker.

"Where are you?" she asked.

"On our way to the airport to pick up Raphael."

"Delay that. I'll send someone for him. We found Odette."

Fifteen

We arrived at the scene just after three in the morning. The highway stretched out before us. Large trees rose up, encasing the area in darkness. The barest hint of light awaited on the horizon. According to folklore, it was the Witching Hour. A time when the veil between the living and the dead was supposed to be at its weakest. I half expected to see Papa Sin standing at the fork in the road, waiting to bargain for souls.

Odette's Prius was parked halfway off the road; the car angled as if it were going to drive through the Welcome to Silverwood sign. Two Silverwood patrol cars blocked the scene, blue and red lights flashing across the roadway and spilling into the grass medium in the center of the highway. An officer stood in the road, outside the yellow crime scene tape, waiting to direct traffic around the incident. A crime scene mobile unit van had parked haphazardly in front of Odette's vehicle.

Chief Declouette's gray Buick was parked just outside the crime scene tape. She stood near Odette's car talking to one of the techs. At our approach, she looked up and signaled for us to park behind her.

A knot of anger and sadness had settled in my gut. I always cried at times like this. When I'd messed up so badly that I couldn't visualize a way to amend my mistake. Hindsight always provided clarity, but in this case, nothing I did would have stopped the inevitability. Odette hadn't been completely forthcoming with us. If she had, maybe. Just maybe. We could have saved her.

Swallowing the emotion lodged in my throat, I climbed into the early morning heat. My vision wavered and the world around me seemed to tilt sideways. I grabbed the car door to stop myself from falling. I was still off balance. Or was it the world around me? Could I still be going in the wrong direction?

"Detectives," the chief called.

Gautier came around the car and stopped in front of me. "You okay?" he asked in a whisper.

I nodded. "Let's get this done."

He stared at me for a minute. Then after a beat started for the chief, with me following behind him to shield myself from her view.

"It's not your fault, Detective Monroe," she said, her hands resting on her hips. It looked as if she had just gotten out of bed with her hair in a loose ponytail instead of the tight one she wore at work. She wore a plain T-shirt and loose denim pants. It was strange to see her not wearing her signature pant suit.

We stopped in front of her and Gautier shifted to the side. "I know," I said.

She studied my face. "Do you?"

I nodded and looked away. I couldn't take her scrutiny

right now. My own self-incrimination was enough. *I should have figured this out sooner.*

"Detective Gautier," the chief said in greeting.

"Ma'am."

"Let's get this done so they can clear the scene." She turned toward the scene. "Odette's been taken to the morgue in Silverwood. I had to wrestle with jurisdiction due to her body being found on the border of Silverwood and Savannah. The chief from Savannah just left." She paused and took a breath. Strain showed on her face. She stared out at the activity, head shaking.

Silverwood sat to the east of Savannah and Statesboro. A single road led into our town. But the sign announcing it was a mile out and yes, given the location of the vehicle, jurisdiction could have gone to Savannah.

"I had the scene videoed and photographed for you to view back at the station," she continued, then pointed at an unfamiliar officer standing off to the side drinking from a Styrofoam cup. "That's Patrolman Marks from Savannah." She signaled for him to join us. "He can walk you through the events. Once you've had a chance to look over the scene, I want you back at the station for a debrief. Detective Sinclair will meet you two there." She gave us one last hard look and then headed toward the officer directing traffic.

The patrolman walked over to us. A middle-aged man in decent shape with a few streaks of gray in his dark brown hair, he walked with a slight limp.

"Marks?" I extended my hand when he stopped in front of us. "I'm Detective Monroe. This is Detective Gautier."

He shook both our hands. "Ma'am, sir." He yawned. "Forgive me. I was at the tail end of my shift when I came upon a Ms...." He pulled a notebook from his front pocket.

"Ms. Palmer's vehicle here." He jerked his chin toward Odette's car. "At first, I believed she might have been in an accident or in need of medical attention. But when I arrived at the driver's window, I saw the blood on the side of her face." He slipped his notebook back in his pocket and started for the car. We followed.

At the car, he glanced at the techs and, after receiving a nod of approval, stepped closer to the driver's side, his boots crunching on the bits of glass in the road. "I attempted to enter the vehicle using a Slim Jim. When that didn't work, I had to break the glass."

He pulled a small flashlight from his back pocket and handed it to me. I examined the ground under the light.

"I checked for a pulse on the victim. When I didn't get one, I called for an ambulance."

"Did you run the plates before you approached the car?" I asked, moving closer to the door. I crouched and studied the bits of glass on the carpet by the seat lever. The car had a strange smell emanating from it that reminded me of industrial cleaner and incense.

"I did. But given the time of night, I didn't wait for a response. Especially since she wasn't moving." He yawned again.

"What direction were you coming from?" Gautier asked.

He pointed north. "I patrol the 16 all the way up to the 404."

I stood. "What shift do you work?" I asked.

"Mid shift. Four days a week," he said.

So, four in the afternoon to one AM. He wasn't very forthcoming, and I didn't feel like standing here, pulling bits and pieces of information out of him for the next hour. "One last question. Were you on shift Monday and Tuesday?"

"I was off Monday," he said.

I nodded. Odette said she'd been driving all night. Which meant she would have come through here early Tuesday morning. "Okay. I'll let you get going. If you can send your notes to the precinct and have the person who worked this shift Monday contact us, that'd help."

"Your chief said you've been looking for Ms. Palmer for a few days. The BOLO came through when the plates were returned."

"That's true," Gautier said.

"Who do you suspect killed her?" he asked, now suddenly ready to converse.

"We're working on it," I said, then waved to one of the crime techs standing by the van. He came jogging over. "I need to get a look at the images you took of Ms. Palmer in the car, and I'll also need a few pairs of gloves." I had developed a habit of using different gloves at each point of contact to prevent contamination.

He strode off, and I turned to the patrolman, who seemed interested now that he wasn't being questioned. "Do you have anything more to add?"

He shook his head. "No. Just wanted to make myself useful. Chief also wanted me to stay just in case you find a reason for Savannah to take over." He yawned again. "But I'm too damn tired, so..." He took one last look around. "This is my cue to leave. I'll get my notes typed up and sent over."

We thanked him and he walked away just as the crime scene tech returned with my requested items. I flipped through the images of Odette sitting in the driver's seat, her head titled to the side and blood pooling around her neck. I didn't know what I expected to see, but something about the image bothered me. And it wasn't just the blood running down her face. Or how her death wasn't like the rest of her families. It felt...

"She's been staged," I said, finally noting the way her hands rested on her thighs. Even her hair seemed to have been styled just right. "She seems posed, like in a portrait."

Gautier stared down at the image. "Why the change in pattern?"

I thought about it. Could we have been chasing something that wasn't true? "Maybe the real crime was Odette's murder and all the others...happenstance?"

Gautier sighed. "I don't believe that." I looked up at him. "And neither do you. My guess? Odette became a problem for..." he trailed off.

"For Tamara," I finished for him. We had no definitive proof of her guilt, only assumptions based on circumstantial evidence. And even that was extremely thin and involved huge leaps to conclusions.

I handed Gautier the camera and pulled on gloves. The car interior had been stripped clean. Blue fingerprint powder covered the steering wheel, gear shift, navigation system and console. "We need to download the history for this," I said, pointing at the system. I opened the center console and found debris and dust. Then I bent and searched the storage compartment underneath and found the same.

"Not much of a back seat," Gautier said.

The floor had the same remnants of dirt. "She wasn't too particular about her car's cleanliness either."

I started to ease out of the car, then stopped. "How tall would you say Odette was?" I asked, staring at the driver's seat.

"A little over five feet," he said, coming to stand next to me.

"The seat is pushed all the way back," I said. "Which meant the last person to drive it had to be well over six feet."

"You think Tamara is that tall?"

"We can check," I said and walked around to the back of the vehicle. The trunk had been left open and a strange metallic scent wafted from inside. I stared down at the immaculate space, thinking. "I'm wondering if the killer put Odette in the trunk." I bent down and inhaled. Yes, definitely some sort of cleaning agent had been used.

"Let's see what they found in the car," I said, pulling off my gloves.

We strode toward the van. The chief had left, leaving only a few techs still combing the area around the car. One tech stood by the back door of the van, holding a tablet in his gloved hand. He glanced up at our approach.

Tall, with dark black hair and a thin mustache, the tech seemed to be in his late twenties. "Detectives," he said. "How can I help?"

We both dipped our heads in greeting. "What did you find in the car?" I asked.

He set the tablet down on the van floor and pulled a crate forward, so it rested at the edge. "Only a few personal items and"—he reached in the crate—"a pile of scarfs."

Gautier and I shared a look. "Scarfs."

He handed me the evidence bag. I studied the bright pieces of fabric. What was the deal with the scarfs? Gautier pulled out another evidence bag and looked at its contents through the plastic. "Her purse and keys," he said.

I was still focused on the scarfs. I was missing something, damnit.

A cold wind blew across my skin. Once again, the world seemed to sway. I looked up and found both Gautier and the tech frozen in place.

"Beatrice Monroe," a deep melodious voice called out.

I followed the sound and found Papa Sin standing at the crossroads.

Sixteen

❧

e wasn't alone. Another man stood on the exact spot where the two roads met, his bloody hands clasped in prayer. I didn't move at first. I was too afraid of acknowledging what couldn't possibly be there. I glanced around and found the officers and tech team also frozen in mid activity as if time had suddenly stopped. Some had their mouths open as if they were about to speak.

"They are there. You are here," Papa Sin said, dark eyes watching me.

"Where am I?" I asked, still not moving. How could he hear me? How could I hear him? He was so far away. Yet right next to me at the same time, whispering in my head.

"In the space between time and reality." Papa Sin didn't offer any further explanation instead he just stood there, watching me. I stepped around Gautier and slowly made my way toward him.

"You pulled me to this place," I said.

He dipped his head, eyes till trained on me. Those dark

depths seemed to pierce my soul. "We are existing in the same place."

Again, I heard him clearly, but he seemed so far away. A car horn sounded, and I whipped around to find the highway deserted.

"You will not reach me," Papa Sin said.

"Please. Is anyone there?" the man at the crossroads asked.

"Who is he?" I asked, trying to make out the man's face, but it was a void filled with darkness and shadows.

"He is not your concern," Papa Sin said. Then he addressed the man. "I am here." The sound of his voice seemed all encompassing, like standing in a wind tunnel.

"Why am I off balance?" I asked, even though so many more questions rested on my lips.

"You know why."

"It wasn't like this before," I said.

"Before was different."

"What makes this time different?" I asked, even though I knew deep down what his answer would be.

"Twins. The soul of a Champion must remain whole. When split, it creates a gateway for pure evil to be born into your world. Once here, twins with Champion blood must remain intact. When one is gone, it creates a chasm in the balance. But only the Champion bloodline can cause this."

"Please, just take my soul and hide me, please!" the man begged.

Papa Sin smiled. "Restore the balance," he said, then turned toward the praying man and added, "What will you give me?"

Reality snapped back into place. "How?" I yelled.

"What?" Gautier responded.

I blinked. I stood in the same spot, as if I hadn't moved. Both Gautier and the tech stared at me, eyes wide. I looked toward the crossroads. Papa Sin was gone.

Seventeen

꧁꧂

We arrived at the station just as the sun crested the horizon. Seeing Papa Sin at the crossroads confirmed my suspicion. My role as a Champion did have significant implications for the case. It was just too bad Papa Sin hadn't given me all the answers I needed. And while he did confirm that Oleatha was still alive, it raised more questions as to why the balance hadn't shifted when the other twins had died.

A few patrol officers stood around the precinct, enjoying coffee before they headed out for their early morning patrol. The detectives were always the last to arrive unless they had an open case. Gautier made a beeline for the breakroom coffee, and I walked to my shared partner's desk.

Raphael sat in his chair, head bowed eyes closed, wearing a crumpled light blue shirt with a stain on the left sleeve. He stirred when I walked up.

"You didn't sleep on the plane?" I asked, taking a seat.

"I was having a meaningful discussion with a toddler while his mother drooled on my arm," he said, eyes still closed. "I now know the meaning of life is Batman and eating cookies." He cracked open one eye. "Bee, seriously. Did you walk here?"

"I look that bad, huh?"

He straightened; his blood shot gaze fixed on me. "What happened?"

Since I'd already told Gautier about my encounter with Papa Sin, I didn't wait to fill Raphael in. Only I didn't stop there. I laid out all the events since we'd parted ways the day before. The story came out in a manic flow and at some point, Gautier had set a bottle of water down in front of me. When I'd finished, I drained the bottle and got up.

"Give me a minute," I said. "I need your keys," I told Gautier. He handed them to me, and I went to get my toiletry bag from the car.

Part of my leaving was due to the emotional turmoil suddenly taking up too much space inside of me. The other reason was I had no doubt my partner was right. I looked terrible. And I smelled terrible, too.

After grabbing a change of underwear and a new shirt along with my toiletry kit, I went inside the precinct bathroom, locked the door, then slid to the floor and closed my eyes.

Even as a rookie, I had always been sure of my ability to solve any case that landed on mine and my partner's desk. Had a knack for sifting through bullshit and finding the right path to take. The right line of questioning needed to get to the truth. Cases were like puzzles and I excelled at solving them. In every one of them my gut instincts had never failed me. Yet here I was, swimming in a sea of confusion as to what I needed to do next.

Yes, I could admit part of my feeling adrift was due to

lack of sleep. But mostly it was the cryptic conversation with Papa Sin and that deep down intuition of something being off. Like the entire answer was right in front of my face, but I just couldn't see it.

Someone knocked on the door.

"Just a minute," I called, surging to my feet. I couldn't break down now. We were no closer to solving this case, and I feared our leaving Silverwood had given the killer the opportunity she needed. Yes, I still believed Tamara was responsible. She was the only one who fit the profile. The only one who would have held a grudge against the family.

It took me a few minutes to clean myself up and comb my hair. I hated being sticky. But that I could deal with. It was going back out there to face my mistake that was bothering me even more. But wallowing wasn't going to do any good. So, after I changed my shirt and underwear, I went out to rejoin the others.

The other staff had arrived since I'd been in the bathroom. They stood, congregated in groups, drinking coffee and chatting. The receptionist was on the phone talking to someone in that tone she saved for when she had to explain something more than once. Sergeant Dennis stood at the counter reading the newspaper and the chief sat on the corner of my desk with her own cup of coffee, still wearing the same clothes I'd seen her in earlier.

"You all ready?" she asked when I stopped in front of them.

"Yes, ma'am," I said.

We followed her into the office, and each of us took a seat. I glanced over at Gautier. His eyes were rimmed in red and a five o'clock shadow was now evident on his face. He'd done all the driving on this trip. I felt bad about putting that burden all on him. But I also knew it wouldn't have been safe for me to drive while experiencing bouts of vertigo, either.

"Sorry," I said.

He stared at me, confusion etched around his eyes. "For what?"

"I should have helped drive. Or at least paid for us to fly back."

He snorted. "Flying would have taken longer. Check in. Travel time to and from the airport. Not to mention we had our service weapons with us. Too much of a hassle." He took another long sip of his coffee. At this rate, he'd be up for days.

"Well," the chief cut in on a sigh filled with fatigue. "While I know ya'll need some rest, we gotta get on the same page with this investigation before I send you home." She glanced at Gautier. "Ease up, detective."

He nodded a little too enthusiastically.

"Shouldn't we continue working on the case now?" Raphael asked. "We have a confirmed murder."

"In any other circumstance, I'd agree with you. Oh, I'd insist you grab a nap at least, but now." She sighed again. "Now, I'm gonna have to call in the FBI."

"Why? We've done all the work. The murder took place here," I demanded. I was not going to let our efforts go in vain. I needed to fix this.

She lifted a hand. "I know. It's not the outcome I wanted either. But if we are dealing with a serial killer, then they've crossed state lines. The case has to go to the Feds. There's no way around it."

"But the other deaths haven't been proven to be murder," I said.

"No. But the totality of what you all have discovered

suggests it is. The sooner we get them involved, the sooner more resources and manpower can be dedicated to apprehending the suspect. Now take me through everything."

"You think they'll let us stay on the case?" Gautier asked.

"I'm going to fight for just that. But I need all your work lined up in such a way that your involvement is necessary. Walk me through it."

We each took her through our interviews and gave her the reports we gathered on the other members of the family.

"Tamara Wright," the chief said. "How sure are you that she's your suspect?"

I thought about it for a minute. "Not completely. But everything fits."

The chief stared at the reports in front of her. "I'll need your written reports by the end of the day. We need to try to reach Odette's sister again and if that fails, we'll have to contact the family in Mississippi. They would be the next of kin."

"What about Odette's ex-husband?" I asked.

She shook her head. "They're divorced. Which leaves the responsibility to the sister to identify the body and make the necessary arrangements." She sighed, shaking her head. "I need to reach out to the detective handling the missing person's case for Tamara and share our concerns." She looked at Raphael. "See if her ex-wife is able to expand on her statement. Maybe coming at this from a different angle will jar more memories." She paused, then said, "You said there was some concern at Odette's work. Did you pick up on anything that would suggest someone there had a grudge against Odette?"

Raphael shook his head. "Just the strange encounter

when I left. Otherwise, I got the impression it had more to do with something she wrote or investigated."

"I'll have one of the officers pull all her articles. Maybe there's a motive in there. We don't want to jump the gun." She paused, then added, "I'm going to alert the FBI, lay everything out. Let them know we're looking into Odette's past and give them what we have on the other family members. I'll give them the opportunity to make the decision. This way, we cover ourselves."

I breathed a sigh of relief.

Her phone rang, and she swiped it up. "Yes, Charlie." Pause. "Okay. We'll be right down." She got up. "Charlie's ready with a preliminary report. Raphael, give Officer Clark the contact information for Odette's sister and her last employer." She stopped in the doorway. "On second thought, let's see if we can reach her ex-husband as well. Maybe their divorce wasn't as straightforward as she implied. We can arrange a remote interview this time."

"And Tamara?" I asked.

"We'll continue to work that angle," she said.

ODETTE PALMER'S NAKED BODY LAY PRONE ON THE steel examination table, head resting in a body block. A white sheet covered the middle section of her body, leaving the arms and legs exposed.

Next to her, a small rolling table sat with a gleaming bone saw, scalpel, and rib shears laying on top. All tools ready to cut open the woman who I'd interviewed just a few days ago.

I swallowed the useless guilt again and concentrated on the sounds of Prince's "The Cross" playing in the background. It was at that moment I understood why Charlie played music. Not necessarily his obsession with Prince, but the reason he kept the place filled with song. Confronting death and the knowledge of your own eventual future in a sterile and cold environment could drain the hope out of anyone. Maybe the music helped push those dark thoughts away and allow him to live in a cocoon of imagined immortality.

We had given Charlie the medical examiners' reports for Mary and Vanessa, and he sat on his stool, studying them alongside the others he had collected. His assistant continued to lay out tools and set up the area to start the autopsy.

I fought a yawn. Eyes watering as I swallowed down the urge. The temptation to close my eyes for just a moment was so great, I feared even a long blink would have me passing out across the floor.

I'd hoped the anger at Odette being murdered would infuse some energy into my body, but the knowledge only left me feeling empty and cold. Like the room I currently stood in.

I glanced at the others. Raphael kept shutting his eyes, each slow blink lasting a little longer. Gautier held his fourth cup of coffee with a crazed caffeine-induced mania in his eyes. The chief looked as if she were ready to scream.

"There is a pattern," Charlie said and stood, effectively pulling me out of my thoughts. "But without the exact means of how these women were murdered, it will be hard to prove. Like I said before, the deaths would have to be classified as suspicious in order for additional toxicology tests to be run." He paused, eyes on the reports. "Given the pattern of deaths as well as this young lady's unfortunate demise, I can push for the additional test."

"Is it enough to get an exhumation order for Ms. Albright?" the chief asked. It was rare for the chief to even attend autopsies. This case must have been wearing on her as well.

Charlie cocked his head to the side, mouth screwed up as if he were chewing on the answer. "I can word it in a way that gives you enough to take to old judge Dixon. No guarantee it will work. But I'm willing to try. We might have to get Dwayne to sign off on it. As for the others, next of kin will have to be notified. I can speak with the coroners who wrote these reports and see if they're willing to update the classification to suspicious. That should get the ball rolling."

The chief nodded.

Charlie looked down at Odette. "As for Ms. Palmer, my preliminary findings are homicide." He pulled on a pair of gloves and twisted Odette's head to the side so that the back of her head faced us. "Here," he pointed at the base of Odette's skull. "She was struck repeatedly in this area, leaving behind four half-moon indentations. Once I remove the brain, I'll get a plaster cast of the marks." He looked up at us. "It will help identify the object." He reset her head back on the block. "So, death by blunt force trauma that likely led to internally bleeding."

"Did the blows break the skin?" I asked, thinking about the pictures of her in the car with a pool of blood resting in the groove on her shoulder blade.

"Yes." He pointed at a spot on her neck. "A thin sharp object pierced her neck here. Could be an injection site. I'll know more when I open her up. But best guess, she was injected with something. I will send off blood and urine samples to toxicology to confirm. He lifted one of her arms. "I found ligature marks around her wrists and ankles that suggest she may have been restrained. Further testing will give me more details on this."

His assistant walked over and handed me a small vial with a thin piece of thread inside. "That was found embedded in her left ankle. I'll have to send it out for analysis, but the material has characteristics of rope or twine."

"What's that in the corner of her mouth?" Gautier asked.

Charlie started nodding and signaled for his assistant. The man handed Gautier another vial, this one filled with white flakes.

"I found trace amounts of purge fluid around the mouth and back of the throat. I'll be sending it along with the blood samples for analysis. I can give you my full report in a few weeks. But for now, I'm comfortable with the findings."

"Any way to move those tests up?" the chief asked.

"Not unless you find some more money. They don't have enough personnel working in the lab to keep up with the workload for the five counties they cover."

"Do you have a time of death?" the chief asked.

Charlie nodded and pulled the sheet to one side, exposing a reddish bruise on her hip. "Given the signs of livor mortis on the skin, Odette died while lying on her side. She was moved after rigor mortis set in. Putting her death between eight and ten PM Tuesday night."

I sucked in a breath. Everyone looked at me. "So, she was..."

"She had to have been taken shortly after Amina's daughter saw her," Gautier said, covering my reaction and my inability to formulate a response to hide it.

"Yes," the chief said, her gaze going to me again. "I need you all to lock down the timeline. Get Ms. Albright's foster son in here to give a formal statement along with Ms.

Albright's neighbor, Amina, and her daughter. I want every second of Odette's time in Silverwood accounted for down to the minute, if possible."

"Yes, ma'am," we said in unison.

"Will you all be staying—"

Someone's phone rang, cutting Charlie off.

Raphael pulled his cellphone from his pocket. "Detective Sinclair," he said. "Oh, yes. Ms. Oleatha. Thank you for returning my call." He paused, looking at us. The chief jerked her head toward the door, signaling for him to take the call outside. "Can you hang on for just a moment?" he asked, walking toward the doors.

"You two go with him. I'll stay for the postmortem," the chief said. "Once you've spoken to the sister, I want you all to go home and get some rest and be back here by two."

We started to walk away and before I got to the door, the chief called out to me.

"Detective Monroe," she said, then turned to Charlie. "We'll be using your office for a minute."

"That's fine, Barbara."

"It's chief...never mind."

I followed her down the short hallway to Charlie's small office. Once we were inside, she shut the door and signaled for me to take a seat. "It's time for you to tell me what your connection is to this case."

I just stared at her.

"I can save you the trouble of calling me insensitive, even go so far as to confirm I am ambushing you when you're vulnerable. But I don't have time for niceties, and you know my character. What I'm doing is disgusting. But it is necessary." She paused. "Sam Gutherie and Steven Ray."

I gasped.

"There it is." She stared at me, waiting. I didn't want to talk about this right now. She was right. It was unfair of her to ambush me in this way. But I also knew my reaction in the morgue hadn't gone unnoticed.

I sighed, swallowing the emotion rising in my throat. She didn't look at me as if she wanted to reprimand me. She stared at me as if she needed to understand.

"Again," she said, staring at me. "I'm not the enemy here, Detective Monroe. It is my job to take care of all of you. And I can't do that when you withhold the truth." Her face softened. "Talk to me."

The flood gates opened and when they did, I couldn't stop myself from telling her everything. From my role as a Champion to my grandmother's journal and my recent encounter with Papa Sin.

When I was done, she got up and pulled tissues from the box Charlie kept on his file cabinet and handed them to me. I cleaned my flushed face.

"Remind me one day to tell you about my first case as a rookie being called to a scene of pure chaos and finding the agent of said chaos standing in the middle of twelve bodies," she said, sitting back down.

She went silent, staring as if deep in thought.

"It seems to me that the messages you kept getting meant the killer was here in Silverwood the whole time," she said the words, as if she were working it out as she talked. "Odette Palmer was an investigative reporter. I find it hard to believe she didn't go looking into some of this."

"I agree," I said.

"And then there's her behavior after talking to you all. I think you're right. She knew someone was after her. My guess, she wanted to confront them on her own. And only reported in case something went wrong."

"And it ended up getting her killed."

"I'll get Tamara's picture out there. Take it to Lewis' Catfish and Po Boys. Word will spread like wildfire if I leave it with Ms. Nettie Mae, and the entire town will be looking for Tamara."

"Is that wise?" I asked.

"We have to start somewhere. And what we need right now are sightings. We don't tell anyone what she's done. Only ask if folks have seen her around town."

I worried about mob justice, but figured the chief knew what she was doing. And we could use the help. Asking everyone in town if they'd seen Tamara would take over a month.

"Now, get home. Get cleaned up. Get some rest and then come back in, ready to do the work."

"You mean the work I should have done in the first place?"

She narrowed her eyes. "You did exactly what anyone in your position would have done. Exactly. You uncovered the Ruby Burkett connection, which led to Tamara as a possible suspect. I'd expect you to follow that lead. If you'd told me before you all set out, I would have suggested the same course of action. Raphael takes good notes. Read up on Odette. Use that mind of yours to work through all the possibilities. Someone wanted her dead. Someone targeted that family. She stood up. "I'll go observe. The preliminary report should be ready when you get back."

I stood up and, unsure what to say, shook her hand. She laughed.

"Get some rest, detective."

"Yes, ma'am."

Eighteen

My first stop when Gautier dropped me at home was the shower. Washing up in the precinct bathroom only went so far. I needed to get the grit and sweat off my skin to really focus.

Once clean, I pulled on some clothes and went to make myself a cup of coffee. I'd confirmed the spells of vertigo were in fact related to my role as a Champion, and until I restored the balance, it wasn't going anywhere. Might as well get the caffeine to give me the energy I needed to do my work. Because I doubted sleep would come easy.

I fixed myself a bagel and took it, along with my coffee, into the front room where my home desk sat. My living room still hadn't been set right, but that was okay. The information on the whiteboards would help me as I walked through all the events since Tuesday.

What I told the chief was right. I should have started my investigation the right way. Like I always did. Compiling information on all the people involved.

But she was right also in that I had been given an opportunity to learn more about myself and even with hindsight; I doubt I'd have done anything different. Didn't stop me from berating myself, though. Because I should have been the one interviewing Odette's former co-workers. I should have been the one talking with Tamara's ex-wife. I trusted Raphael took good notes. He always did. But I preferred to observe the person I was interviewing.

After finishing my bagel, I plugged my phone into my laptop and started the program to inscribe my interview with Odette. I left the volume on low as I pulled up another program and recorded the date and time we first encountered Odette Palmer.

Most cops hated paperwork. I didn't particularly love it either. But there was something almost hypnotic about writing up the events as I remembered them. It helped put me back in that time and space, and occasionally it jarred small details I might have overlooked in the first place. In this case, it was Odette's clothes.

I sat back and stared at my notes from my interview with Amina's daughter. Why had Odette changed clothes? I thought back to earlier this morning when I viewed the pictures taken at the crime scene. I hadn't paid too much attention to what she was wearing in the photo. I was more fixated on the blood.

I picked up the phone and called Officer Clark. "Clark," he answered.

"Hey, Clark. It's Monroe."

"Shouldn't you be resting?" he said, a teasing note in his tone.

"Yeah, I'll rest when the case is solved. Right now, I need to know what you've got on Odette Palmer. I also need copies of the photos from the crime scene and any notes you have from Sinclair. Well, any you were able to decipher."

"That's a tall order. Sinclair's notes aren't legible and all I managed were a few names of people he spoke with at Sun Crest Tribune. I can email you the photos from the crime scene. And I did manage to get the address and phone number for her ex-husband. He hasn't returned my call. Ran the usual background checks on Odette. She came back clean. I have an intern searching through her social media. Most of it is pictures of places. Nothing political or confrontational."

"What about all her old articles?"

"Can't find any of them."

I thought about that for a minute. Raphael had said her coworkers had seemed almost reluctant to talk to him about Odette. He'd even suggested their reluctance, as well as them being forced to sign an NDA could have been attributed to something she wrote. Taking all her stories offline meant that must have been true. "Okay, thanks. Send everything else over for me."

"Will do. Now, get some rest."

I snorted and hung up.

I needed Raphael's notes. No, I really needed him to translate them. Odette's voice cut through my thoughts, and I turned up the volume on my phone.

Two months ago, my editor pulled me into his office and told me the paper was looking to rebrand. He said he wanted to bring in fresh new perspectives. My whole career had been spent doing just that. I never once stopped growing. But it wasn't my writing that was the problem. It was my age. And the money I was making. These "fresh new faces" came with a substantial cut in salary. So, I grabbed my stuff and walked out. Didn't shed not one damn tear. Not until I got home, at least.

Why had she lied about her job? I pulled up the website for the paper and checked the time. They were a few hours behind us, making it nine in the morning. I scrolled down the page until I came across a telephone number, then picked up the phone and called.

"Sun Crest Tribune, how may I direct your call?"

"Good morning. My name's Detective Beatrice Monroe from the Silverwood Police Department. I'm looking for Mrs. Hainsworth."

"What is this regarding?" the woman asked hesitantly.

"I'll need to discuss that with her."

She didn't respond right away. A minute later, a woman picked up and spoke. "Detective Monroe? This is Grace Hainsworth. We already talked with a Detective Sinclair from your department and I'm afraid we have nothing further to add." There was a briskness in her tone that suggested she was on the verge of hanging up.

"I understand that," I said in a rush before she could. "I was wondering if the circumstances of the NDA everyone signed survive after death."

"Excuse me?"

"I don't mean to be blunt. But Odette Palmer is deceased. It is imperative we get a clear picture of who she was."

"If I'm to understand you. You're saying Odette was murdered?"

"No ma'am. I'm saying she's deceased. Why would you suggest murder?"

"I highly doubt you'd be calling about her death if she died of natural causes, detective."

"Fair enough. But I can't confirm that. I just need—"

"Look," she said, cutting me off. "I'm sorry for her family, but I've said all I can say about Odette Palmer."

"Would it be better if I obtained a subpoena?"

"You don't have jurisdiction in Los Angeles, detective. Our answering your partner's questions was a courtesy. One we don't plan on extending again without a warrant," she said and hung up.

"Crap!"

I leaned back in my chair and stared at the screen. The only other option we had in getting information from her old employer was the woman who had asked for Raphael's phone number. I wished he had gotten hers in return. There had to be reason she wanted it, and I only hoped that reason led her to contact us. Sooner rather than later.

My message notification chimed. I received three emails simultaneously. I opened the one from Clark and clicked on the attached images from the crime scene. She was wearing the same clothes she'd worn at the precinct. Which meant she had changed four times. Why? And what had happened to her other clothes?

Next, I skimmed through his notes. Nothing different from what he'd told me over the phone. Except he didn't mention the BOLO put out for Tamara. That must have been the chief's doing.

I sighed heavily; the gesture morphed into a yawn. I needed sleep. I was circling the same information, hoping to find just one little kernel of information to help me understand.

I laid my head on my desk and closed my eyes. I needed to narrow down my focus. Concentrate on finding Tamara and...

Someone pounded on my door at the same time my notification bell sounded. I snapped up from my chair, and the world swam in front of me. "Shit," I said aloud and stumbled to go answer the door.

Raphael stood in the doorway, his face morphing from fear to confusion. "Did you not hear your phone?" he asked, stepping inside.

"What time is it?" I asked. My mind was still foggy. I hadn't meant to fall asleep.

"It's almost four. The chief sent me to get you." He took in the room. "Did you even make it to the bed or did you work till you dropped?"

I stared at him.

"Worked." He sighed. "Well, Oleatha is here. She got to the precinct just after three." He walked into the kitchen. "Everyone did a double take. Her resemblance to Odette is uncanny."

"They're twins," I said, gathering my notes and shoving them into my laptop bag. "Of course they're going to look alike." I paused. "Exactly?"

He came back into the room with a soda in his hand. "No. Oleatha wears her hair short and has a more reserved sense about her. It's kinda creepy, though. The way she just kept sizing everyone up."

"Did she seem sad?"

He twisted his mouth up. "Not broken up. But definitely...hurt. Like she's holding it all in."

They were estranged. "Give me a minute. I gotta change and brush my teeth."

He nodded and sat down heavily on my office chair.

We arrived at the station twenty minutes later to find Oleatha in the chief's office talking to Gautier and the chief. Raphael was right, it was a bit uncanny seeing the woman sitting there looking so much like her sister. Despite the haircut, they were the same.

"Detective Monroe," the chief said. "This is Mrs. Oleatha Carmichael."

She turned to look at me and when our eyes met, a chill ran down my spine.

When one is gone, it creates a chasm in the balance.

She stared at me, eyes filled with confusion. "Are you okay, detective?" she asked, a note of concern in her voice.

I cleared my throat. "Yes. I'm fine, it's just..."

She let out a soft laugh. "Yeah. I've been getting looks since I arrived." She blew air through her lips and dabbed at the side of her eye. "Your chief has taken me to see my sister. I never thought we'd run out of time."

The chief signaled for me to sit. I took the seat next to Oleatha. "I understand," I said. I started to pull my phone out, then stopped. Once again, I made the decision not to follow my own routine.

"Do you mind if we record this interview?" Gautier asked.

I could have kissed him.

"Umm...am I a suspect?"

"No. No," the chief said. "Detective Monroe records all her interviews."

Oleatha stared at me for a minute, her gaze going from skepticism to understanding. "Oh, of course. Dyslexia. In that case, yes. That's fine."

I didn't see the need to correct her assumption. I put my

phone on the chief's desk and set it to record. "Thank you," I said.

She dabbed at her eyes again and it gave me a sense of déjà vu. Odette had done something similar when we had talked with her.

"My deepest condolences for your loss."

Her face brightened. "Thank you."

I nodded. "I understand that you and your sister weren't that close. I don't know how much my chief has told you, but we are looking at two possibilities as it relates to your sister's murder."

"Of course."

"The first. She gave us a different story when it came to her employer. She implied she had been let go due to the company wanting to shift to a younger demographic. Yet, our research shows there might have been other issues. Are you aware of anything that might have happened with a coworker or one of the people or organizations she investigated for her articles?"

She shook her head slowly.

"Do you happen to have any of your sister's articles?" Raphael asked.

She shook her head again.

The next question was going to be difficult. But it had to be asked. I just hope she gave us more than a shake of her head.

"Are you aware you have a cousin named Tamara Wright?" I said, carefully.

She nodded.

I looked at Gautier. He moved into her line of sight.

"Can you tell us about her?" he asked.

She looked at him. "Well. I know my Aunt Natalie gave her up for adoption. I also know she had contacted my aunt back in 2019. I didn't talk to her as much as my sister did. Aunt Natalie seemed to be more...fond of her. She was always helping her in some way or another." She sucked in a breath. There was a note of sadness in her voice that wasn't there when she talked about her sister. Did she envy the relationship Odette had with their aunt? "From what I understand," she continued. "Aunt Natalie didn't want anything to do with the child."

"Here's another one of those conflicting stories," I said, happy she had finally started talking. "Your Aunt Cherie implied Ms. Albright blamed her family for making her give up Tamara."

"Really?"

"Yes."

"I never heard that," she said, almost shutting down again.

"How did you hear about Tamara?" Gautier asked.

She looked at him. "Well, I...I believe Odette said something." She shook her head. "I can't remember."

"When would she have mentioned her?" Gautier asked.

She shook her head. "I'm sorry, I just don't remember."

I nodded. That was odd. I'd already assumed Odette had been lying about her knowledge of the girl, but for Oleatha to be so unsure. It just didn't make sense. "Do you feel comfortable talking about your sister?" I asked, changing the subject. "Why were you two so distant?"

She sighed and rested against the seat. "Odette has always been difficult. She isn't the easiest person to get along with. My mother was like that, too. Just...mean? I wanted to have a relationship with her. My girls wanted to be in her life. But she kept us and everyone else except for Aunt Natalie at a distance." Again a note of sadness.

"Your Aunt Cherie says you didn't visit the family often when you were children."

She snorted. "That was my mother's doing. She didn't want us down there. She was very protective. Strict, too. I swore I'd be a better mother to my own kids."

"Was she afraid someone would hurt you all?" I asked, thinking of what had happened to Ms. Albright.

She shook her head. "No. She just was overprotective of Odette. Careful with who she allowed around my sister. She didn't much care what happened to me, though," she said with bitterness in her tone.

I was beginning to understand why she and Odette had a strained relationship and it had nothing to do with how difficult her sister had been.

"Why did you ask about Tamara?" she asked suddenly. "Do you think she killed my sister?"

I blinked. Her tone was so a matter of fact that it threw me for a minute. "We are considering that," I said carefully. "Did she ever tell you her concerns about the members of your family and..."

"That someone was killing them," she said, shaking her head. "She let Aunt Natalie convince her of so many things. I really don't care to go into it. Yes, I've lost quite a few people, including my mother, but I don't believe someone is out to get us." She paused, then continued, "My sister called me and asked for me to check on my aunt before she took off to...I forget where she went. When I called, Aunt Natalie tried to convince me we were being targeted."

"Did she tell you who she suspected?"

She shook her head.

We were back to non-answers. I tried a few more questions before the chief signaled that I should wrap it up. I was straying dangerously close to interrogating her, and that wasn't fair. Despite the strained relationship between her and Odette, I could tell she was upset, and it was best if I waited and gave her the time to grieve.

"Will you be staying in town long?" I asked, standing.

"No. I'm going to catch a flight out tomorrow. We'd planned on taking the girls on a little trip up to see the Redwoods in Northern California for a home school project. I can arrange for her...for her body to be sent back to LA, right?"

"Yes, I will have to confirm with the DA when it can be released."

She stood there, staring at the ground. "You always believe you have all the time in the world to mend fences."

"Yes, we do," the chief said softly.

"Where are you staying?" I asked.

"I need to find a hotel. I would ask Dwayne, but I don't want to burden him."

"I understand. I can recommend the place your sister was staying." I looked at the chief. "Did anyone collect her things from Amina's?"

"Yes," she said. "We can get those to you after the DA gives the okay. Will that work?"

She nodded.

"I'll walk you out and get you that address," Raphael said, ushering her to the door.

Before leaving, she turned and looked directly at me. Again, a chill raced down my spine. "You will let me know when you find the person who did this, right?"

I nodded.

She smiled and walked out the door.

"Please tell me you got an alibi for Oleatha," I said, retrieving my phone from the desk. The woman had lied repeatedly, and I didn't understand why.

"It was the first thing I did," the chief said. "What is your impression of her?"

"Cold. Jealous. And...I don't know. She just seems..."

"Off," Gautier said, staring at the door. "And has a strange case of selective memory."

We all nodded. I did want to press Oleatha if only to get some straight answers from her about Tamara. Her knowledge of the girl had to have come from her sister or Ms. Albright. And that isn't something to easily forget. So why did she claim she had forgotten?

That man told her she'd birth evil. That twins were broken.

A woman is born with all the eggs she will ever have in her life. Which meant, when Odette and Oleatha's mother was inside her mother's womb. She was carrying the eggs that would one day be fertilized and become the twins.

Had we just met evil?

Nineteen

When everyone had finally gone home, I spread all the evidence on the floor next to my desk and sat on my heels, staring down at it. My focus kept shifting back to Oleatha. And because of this, I looked at the evidence, trying to see her in the thread. But I couldn't picture it. We had yet to reach her husband to confirm her alibi, but she had shown her airline ticket to the chief.

But that didn't mean she wasn't already here Tuesday night.

I looked at the timeline, then did a map search online. It would take a little over thirty-four hours to get from here to Oleatha's house by car. It was doable. She also could have flown home, then turned around and flew back out here. But did I really think she'd killed her sister? She would have had to drive out here with Odette, kill her, then fly back home. If that were the case, Odette would have mentioned her sister coming with her. But then again, Odette had kept a great deal of information from us so... It didn't fit. No matter how I looked at it. It just didn't work.

I sighed and picked up the book. All of this did start with Ruby Burkett. That much I understood. By giving birth to her twins, she introduced the possibility of pure evil being born. But what did that look like?

Yes, Oleatha was cold. Everyone in the room had a similar response to her. She hadn't displayed outright cruelty or hatred. Just a detachment we weren't used to seeing from a person who'd just learned a loved one had been killed. She didn't ask the many questions we usually got. Nor did she place any demands on us to find the killer. Her only comment on it was to let her know when we found the one responsible. But that could just be the estrangement.

"Damnit," I said, getting up. I needed to move for a minute.

A chill had settled in the air. Without everyone inside expelling body heat, the malfunctioning air-conditioning unit actually put out enough cool air to make the place bearable. It was too bad I didn't have a sweater.

I went into the breakroom and flipped on the light. The illumination blazed against the darkness inside the main room. I was only using our desk lamps to look over the case. We had grabbed dinner from Lewis' Catfish and Po Boys after Oleatha left. I put my leftover in the microwave and leaned against the counter, twisting my head side to side to crack my neck while I waited for the microwave to go off.

At the *ding*, I took my shrimp pasta back to my desk to eat. As I shoveled food into my mouth, my gaze settled on the note Odette claimed Ms. Albright had received.

It started with Ruby Burkett and will end with you.

The more I studied it, the more it sounded like someone blamed Ruby for their circumstance. Who did that fit?

Odette was dead.

Her sister, despite the chilly demeanor, didn't seem unhappy about her life. Their Aunt Cherie also seemed content. Their grandpa was angry at losing his wife and the other side of the family wanted nothing to do with anyone.

Tamara Wright was the only outsider here. Yet, the impression Raphael got about Tamara from her ex-wife didn't line up with a murder accusation.

Even my interview with Dr. Aduke Oyenuga at Shared Pain suggested Tamara was looking for a happy reunion. Someone to accept her.

But she *was* the only viable suspect. The only one who could possibly hold a grudge against her birth mother. But what did that have to do with the rest of the family? And why kill twins?

I sighed. Could I be overblowing the situation? Could the deaths be merely coincidence and we just spent the last few days collecting evidence that led nowhere? It was starting to feel that way.

Distraction.

The word settled in my mind. I stared down once again at the accumulated information. All of it led to nowhere. No motive. No means. No opportunity. Just a broken family who had suffered loss.

"Fuck!"

I wasn't getting anywhere because nothing in the case made sense. We had one provable homicide and until something else came up, I would focus on that. I grabbed my to-go container and took it to the trash. Next, I swept up all the notes and stacked them in a pile on my desk. I needed sleep. And to come back with...damnit, fresh eyes.

When I went to close my laptop, my attention snagged on an unanswered email waiting in my inbox. It was from an unfamiliar address with no subject line. I clicked on it and found a single video file attachment. Spam?

"Fuck it," I said and clicked on the video.

The Pasadena Butcher's handsome face filled the screen.

"You're not showing the right amount of emotion. Try again."

"I have to explain why I wasn't at her funeral."

"I don't believe you cared. Try again."

A few minutes into the clip, my blood ran cold. Clarity came like a tidal wave, bowling over me until all I could do was scream.

I picked up the phone and called Charlie.

He answered on the second ring. "What can I do for you?"

I explained to him what I needed and ironically, he had already recorded the information in the postmortem report. I just hadn't read through it. So sure was I that I'd find the answers in all the notes we had. When the answer had been available all this time.

After I hung up with him, I went through my interview with Odette again and when I found the place I needed, I put my phone in my pocket and finished watching the sick video I had been sent. It had been there the whole time. But I kept trying to fit everything into a scenario I knew made no sense. Square peg. Round hole.

It was time to take down evil.

Twenty

W hen I walked into the room, I found her standing by the bed, back to the door, stuffing items into a small duffle bag. I watched her for a minute, trying to figure out how I'd missed those subtle clues about her true identity. Yes, her hair was different. Her clothes too. But those things could be changed. It was our mannerisms that gave us away. And that whole time she sat across from me in the interview room, I'd had the opportunity to study them. It was the main reason I did record interviews.

Yet, I'd missed it. Because the woman standing by the bed had put on a show. One she'd obviously rehearsed numerous times.

"I watched your rehearsal with the Pasadena Butcher," I said in way of a greeting. I was way past tired and didn't feel like playing anymore games.

"Oh," she said, putting a shirt in her bag. She took her time closing it, setting it to the side, then, finally, turning to me. The coldness in her eyes I'd glimpsed in the chief's office was there. "Don't you mean Odette's interviews?"

I let out a dry chuckle, then sat on the chair near the door. "Now, how would you know your estranged sister interviewed a serial killer? Is it the same way you knew about Tamara?"

She covered her mouth and widened her eyes in a sarcastic gesture. "Guess I slipped." She stared at me. "Are you recording this?"

"It didn't help me the first time." I smiled. "But it will help me prove who you are."

"How?" she said, smirking.

I pulled my phone from my pocket and brought up the dictation app, then pressed play.

I confronted him that night. At first, he tried to deny it. But his heart wasn't in the lie, so he broke down and...and started crying. He told me he'd had a vasectomy when he was eighteen years old because he couldn't stand having to watch his baby brother and decided he never wanted kids. Here I was, this gullible love-struck idiot pouring my heart out to a cute boy about the future and all the while he knew that future was impossible. But he loved me so much, he didn't want to lose me. Give me a fucking break.

"The woman in the morgue, your sister, has given birth. But you, *Odette*, have not."

She glared at the phone, then at me. "Fuck you," she gritted out.

I slid the phone back into my pocket. "You never told me one lie. I've listened to this entire interview and my gut told me you were telling the truth." I lifted a finger. "Except the part about the book and Ruby Burkett. Then, something felt... off." I paused, watching her. "Much like it did earlier today. But then I remembered how you talked to Sgt. Dennis. That was the real you."

"If you believe so," she smiled.

I ignored her sarcasm and continued, "An investigative reporter being okay with not knowing about a significant part of her history? No one in your family had the resources you had. The connections. Yet, you insisted you didn't know who Ruby Burkett was."

"How did you get the video?" she asked, ignoring everything else I said.

"Someone sent it to me."

"Who?"

I didn't answer.

"That's why everyone signed an NDA. Because you were being trained by a killer."

"And writing so many compelling articles about my interviews. My editor praised my work. Threw a party in my honor because I'd raised circulation. But then they found my tapes. Mutual Destruction is how I phrased it when they tried to fire me outright."

"How did you kill your family?"

"Tired of hearing about my life?"

"I'm tired of you, Odette Palmer. Now," I stood up. "Tell me."

She lifted her chin. "And what if I don't?"

I shrugged. "Doesn't matter. We have you for your sister's murder."

She shook her head and screamed. "So much of my fucking life wasted!"

"And so much more of it will be spent in jail." I pulled the cuffs from my back pocket. "Odette Palmer, you are under arrest—"

"Fuck you!"

It was too fast. One minute I stood there, cuffs in my hand. The next, a heavy weight slammed into me, and I fell to the floor. It took me a minute to realize it wasn't her, but the duffle bag that hit me.

Her foot hit my side, knocking the wind out of me. I shoved the bag off me and tried to grab her leg as she rushed by, only managing to graze my fingers across her tennis shoes.

I scrambled to my feet, tossing the heavy bag to the floor. My cuffs had skidded across the floor, but I left him there. Pain pulsed down my side from where she had kicked me, and a wave of vertigo-induced nausea flowed through me. I slammed my hand against the wall, trying to regain my equilibrium.

Loud noises floated into the room.

My chest heaved as I took a step towards the door.

She was getting away.

"Leave her alone," a man's voice called out.

Another step.

A high-pitched scream rang out.

I shoved myself at the opening and bit down on the pain. Then I snatched my gun from its holster and half stumbled down the stairs. Only to come to an abrupt stop at the gruesome sight before me. A stranger lay on the ground, holding his bloody side. Odette had somehow managed to get a knife and was now standing behind Amina's daughter with the blade pressed against the young girl's throat.

"Let her go," I slurred, eyes going from Denise to the man on the floor. His chest was still rising and falling.

"I don't think so." She glared at me.

"I will let you walk out." I eased down. Once again the

room spun, and I barely kept myself from falling. "I'm putting my gun on the floor. Just let the girl go."

I heard a sniffle on my right and turned and found Amina on the floor with a tray of food scattered around her, holding her bloody arm.

"You think I'm stupid. The minute I leave, you call it in, and I get caught. I won't go to jail."

"Then how do you see this ending?" I said, keeping my grip on my gun. "You want me to shoot you? Suicide by cop? I won't give you that."

She laughed. "I won't allow you to, either." She licked her lips and looked around the room. "I had planned this so carefully. And you just had to ruin it. I would have been free of the ones who made me broken."

"What?" I asked.

"The man told me I was broken. Aunt Natalie even said so." She sneered. "But she lied to me about her daughter. She knew about the man. She knew what we were and never said a word."

"Where did you meet the man?"

She stared; eyes rounded. "I knew there was reason you were fascinated with that book. You know about Champions." She laughed, the knife slipped, and a tiny wound opened on Denise's neck.

The young girl stared at me, tears streaming down her face.

I stepped forward. "Careful, you're hurting her."

She laughed. "You think I care. I'm not capable of caring."

I shook my head. "I don't believe that. You cared about your aunt."

Her lips thinned. "She lied to me!" she screamed,

pointing the knife at me. "All she had to do was tell the truth."

"But the rest of your family. Your mother. Your sister. Cousins. Grandmother. None of them lied to you. Why would you kill them?"

One of the other guests must have called the police by now.

The man on the floor groaned, and I moved toward him.

"No! You stay there or I will cut her throat."

"I can't let him bleed to death."

"Yes, you can. He shouldn't have gotten in the way. None of them should have."

"Please. Let me go," Denise said.

"Shut up!" Odette pushed the knife closer, drawing more blood.

I raised my gun. "Don't!"

"What are you going to do? Shoot through her?" She pushed the knife further.

I moved, and she stepped back. "I said. Stay there."

Amina crawled into the room and eased up, blood running down her arm. "Let my daughter go, you bitch!"

Odette laughed. "No."

I was missing something. Why didn't Odette just leave? She'd had ample time to do so. Why toy with Denise? Why do any of this?

"What is your endgame?" I asked again.

Fear crept into her eyes. "I don't have one. Except I'm not going to jail."

"That's the only way out."

"Is it?"

I didn't like the resolve in her tone. Nor the cornered rat look in her eyes. She didn't have any options, and she knew it.

I needed to keep her talking. "Tell me about your conversation with the man?"

"*The man*," she said mockingly. "You know who he is."

"Papa Sin," I said. "Tell me what he said to you."

She smiled then. Like her entire existence rested on me asking that one question. But the look in her eyes didn't match the smile. That look...scared me. "Why did I do it? What did he say? Is that what you want to know? Is that what you *need*, Detective Monroe?"

It was too late for me to take it back. The gleam of satisfaction in her eyes broadcast her next move.

"No!" I screamed.

She plunged the knife into Denise's side once, then ripped it out, spraying blood in an arc across the ceiling, then shoved the girl toward me, and drew the blade across her own neck.

She smiled, then hit the floor.

I STARED OUT AT THE SEA OF BLUE AND RED LIGHTS flashing. Neighbors on both sides of Amina's stood in their yard watching. I couldn't move from my spot on the porch. I didn't have the strength to even wipe Denise's blood from my face and hands. I should have been more vigilant when Amina raised concerns about Odette. But honestly, it wouldn't have helped. We all believed it was Oleatha who'd checked into Odette's old room.

Sgt. Dennis walked up and took a seat beside me. It was a little strange seeing him out in the field.

"You knew," I said. "You knew something was wrong with this case." I couldn't look at him. A part of me couldn't face the reality of my mistake in not talking to him sooner.

He stretched his leg out. "Nothing wrong with the case. But something wasn't right about her. It took me thirty years to develop my gut instincts. You're good, Detective Monroe. Better than most. But you're still new to this."

I snorted. "You sound like the chief." We sat in silence for a while. A crime tech walked past us and went into the house. "Is that why you had the case file?"

"Yeah. I was gonna take a look at it. I'd planned to do so when she first called. But you know, there are times, the day just gets away from you."

I turned to him. "I'm sorry."

His eyes narrowed, brows shifting down. "For what? You did your job. Same as anyone. You went with what was presented to you. I don't fault you for being upset. In your shoes, I would have been too. If our jobs were easy and the criminals wore signs pointing to their guilt, they wouldn't need that many of us. Probably get by with one or two."

I chuckled, and he smiled.

"You need to get yourself cleaned up. You didn't discharge your weapon, but you did get into a confrontation with a suspect. There is going to be a slew of useless questions coming your way. Bunch a people asking you why you didn't know when they have the privilege of all the information being laid out for them." He shook his head.

"I can't believe she took her own life," I said. "It seems cowardice."

"You can look at that way. Or you can see it for what we both know to be true."

"That is?"

"A power play. She dies, leaving you with no answers. Meaning she won."

"*Why did I do it? What did he say? Is that what you want to know? Is that what you need, Detective Monroe?*"

"Why didn't you become a detective?" I asked.

He laughed. "Too much damn stress and no set hours. My missus would never have allowed it." He stood and extended his hand to me. "Let's get you cleaned up."

I took his hand and stood. Raphael and Gautier came rushing up the walkway.

"She's fine. It's not her blood," Sgt. Dennis said and walked away.

"Why didn't you call me?" Raphael asked, eyes blazing. "Or backup at least."

I shook my head. "I don't know."

Chief Declouette came walking our way with an unfamiliar man beside her.

"Union rep," Gautier said. "Surprised they have 'em here in Silverwood."

"Detective Monroe. Beatrice," she said. "How are you?"

"I'm okay, ma'am. Just waiting to hear if the victims are okay."

"We can head to the hospital," Gautier said. I looked at him. He knew this was eating me up. It would have been hard to face Amina right now. I'd put her child in danger.

"Thank you, detectives," the chief said. She gave them both a look and then focused on me. "This is Troy Saunders. He's going to walk you through what happens next."

I half listened to the man while I watched my partners walk back to Raphael's truck. No matter what came next, I'd done my job.

And restored the balance.

Twenty-One

M y first day back after a month on administrative leave, I came in to find the full postmortem report for Odette Palmer on my desk. I stared at the folder, anger rising inside of me, then pushed it away and set my brand-new journal in its place.

Amina and her daughter Denise had survived. Her guest did as well. But the fallout from the incident had cost the department money and our chief was still dealing with the legal issues surrounding it. I didn't blame anyone for suing the department. I was just glad Amina had chosen to forgive me. Even though I had yet to forgive myself.

They'd found Oleatha's husband and two girls the day after Odette took her life. She had killed them and left them in the house with the air-conditioning running. Then driven cross country with her sister in the trunk, tied up with rope and scarfs to hide the marks. The fact that Charlie had found ligature marks on Oleatha led me to believe the woman had fought. And when Odette tried to give her the same dose of digitalis, she gave the other family members she killed, Oleatha had thrown it up, forcing Odette's hand.

During my leave, I'd spent my time rewriting my reports on Steven Ray and Sam Guthrie and Odette Palmer. Including in them all the details surrounding my work as a Champion. The time we spent looking for answers about Odette's family hadn't been a complete waste. It did answer questions about how Champions were created. I had to count that as a win. It also exposed me to the effects of what I could expect to feel when the balance was off. Which meant, next time, I'd be prepared.

Now, I just needed to find Tamara.

I picked up my desk phone and dialed the number Raphael had left on my desk. The woman answered on the first ring.

"Sun Crest Tribune, Holly Winters."

"This is Detective Monroe."

"Umm...hello," she said hesitantly.

"Thank you for the video."

"Okay, can I call you back?"

"Don't worry. Our conversation won't jeopardize you. Right now, I want to focus on Tamara Wright."

"Who is she?"

"Her cousin. And I trust you understand who 'her' is."

"Yes...yes, I do. I didn't..." I heard wrestling in the background and then a door closing. "I didn't like the paper not giving those...those tapes to the police," she whispered. "But they were adamant about us keeping quiet. But when your partner showed up asking about *her,* I decided I had to do something. She'd been interviewing him since 2019. The one I sent is not as bad as the others."

"How do you still have them?"

Silence. "I'm the one who found them. I made copies just in case. I can send you the rest, but you can't disclose where you got it."

"Okay." The tapes would provide evidence on Odette's crimes and get the family answers. They might also have some evidence as to what she'd done to her cousin, Tamara. "Now, let's talk about Tamara. I believe she's been killed by *her..*"

Holly gasped.

"And when she died, she took that knowledge with her. We will find Tamara and get closure for her ex-wife and family. And I want you to help me do it."

"How?"

"I'm sending you all the information I have on her. You're an investigative reporter. Dig as deep as you can into her life and the life of Odette. And I will do the same. She had to leave clues somewhere."

"I'll do it," she said softly. There was a note of determination in her voice.

I nodded and leaned back in my chair. "Weekly check-ins?"

"That works for me. Use the email address I sent the video from."

I smiled into the phone. I would not let this story die. They had spent all of two weeks trying to find Tamara Wright in 2019. No media coverage. No documentaries. No podcasts. Just a few doors being knocked on and that was it.

After we hung up, I pulled out the report I'd created for Tamara and opened it. There wasn't much there. But that was going to change. She'd become my own white whale. I started an email to my new partner at the Tribune and looked up when a shadow fell over me.

"How are you holding up, Detective Monroe?" the chief asked, sitting on the edge of my desk. She held a folder in her hand.

"Another case?" I asked, staring at the file.

"In a way. You didn't answer my question."

"Feeling a bit defeated."

She nodded, crossing her arms. "You all grumble so much about my 'fresh eyes' approach to cold cases. That process can work for the current ones as well. You spent so much of your time invested in this situation. Close enough that you couldn't see anything else around you. And, I suspect, you stopped listening to your gut." She paused and stared at me. "Tell me. If you had taken one step back and really looked at Odette Palmer. Really listened and allowed yourself the space to doubt, to question, what do you think you would have discovered?"

"That her story didn't add up. She told a few half-truths, and I chalked that up to grief. But she had us there, Chief. She'd been practicing. But still...she never answered a question where she would have to outright lie. Evade, yes. But not lie. And if not for that sad story of her life she told, I would have called her on it."

"I know you would have. You're a damn good detective." She set the folder on my desk. "Now, let's go close this case out as well."

I opened the folder to find an arrest warrant for the mayor. "What?"

"'Let he who is without sin cast the first stone'. Seems our mayor likes them young. And we finally got enough evidence to show that." She smiled. "Time to go clean house."

I grinned. "Ready when you are."

She got up. "Let me grab Gautier and Sinclair. I feel my

life might be in danger." She winked and went over to the breakroom.

I chuckled and opened my journal. This case may not have gone the way it should have, but it did set me on the right path regarding my origins. I would continue learning and writing it all down for my own descendant. So, she would be prepared for what's to come.

I wrote:

We are born from Sin.

THE BURKETT FAMILY

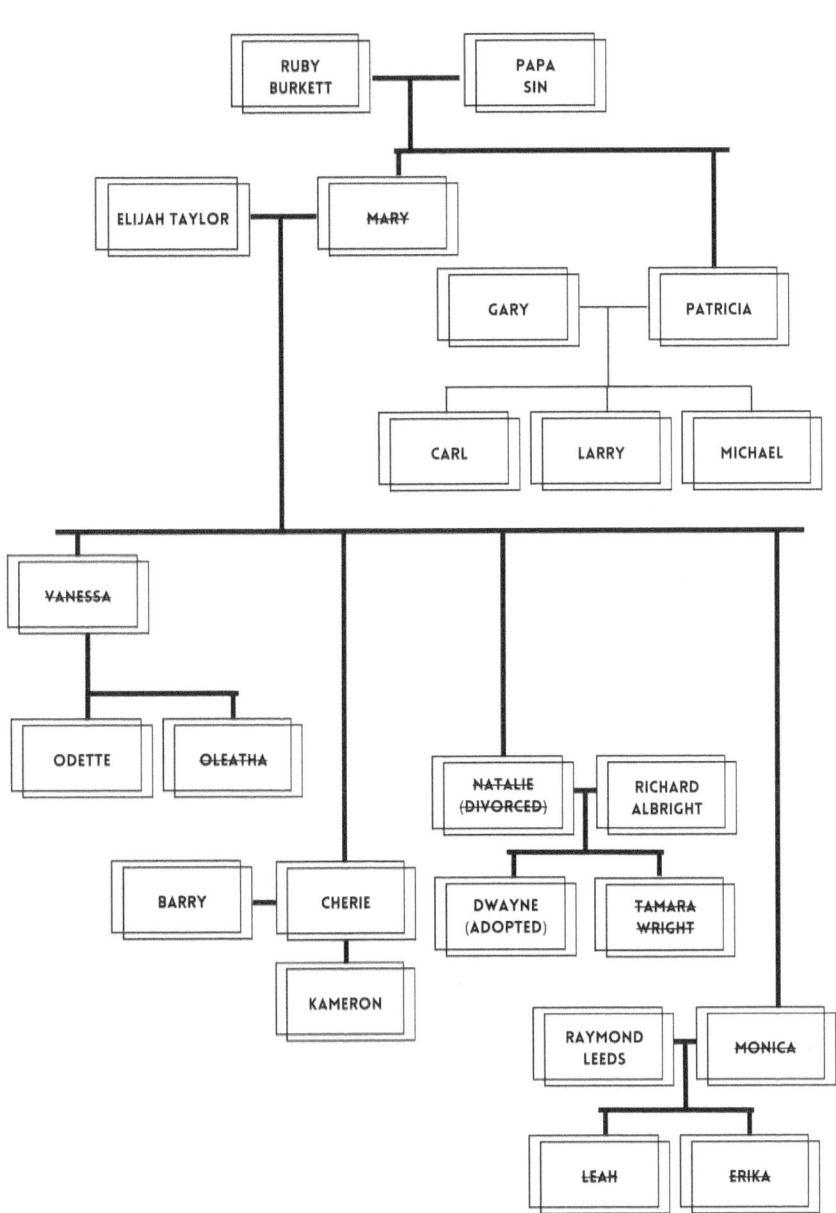

Preview the next book in
A HORDE OF DEAD POETS
collection!

AVAILABLE NOW

One

Truly Butcher was nobody's bitch. Loud? Sure. Obnoxious? Absolutely. Lazy? Uh-huh. But nobody, *nobody*, took advantage of Truly Butcher. So that's why she had been, and continued to be, so pissed about her piece of shit boyfriend of the last three years cheating on her for over half of that time. She cranked the car stereo, and scream-sang Miley Cyrus's "Wrecking Ball" as she sped down route 27. Back to Moss Landing. Back to where she came from.

The song ended and some RV salesman took over the radio waves. Truly stabbed the power button and grabbed her purse. She pulled out a pack of cigarettes and ripped the cellophane off with her teeth. She lit up and took a long drag, sure as hell whatever burned inside damaged her lungs. Though Truly wasn't a long-term smoker, only when the shit hit the fan. And that it did, often enough. She knew cancer would get her in the end, no matter what.

Ever'body gotta die some kinda way, her grammaw used to say.

And when generations of family spent their whole lives

living next to a condemned nuclear processing plant, it was gonna be some kind of cancer-way. Every tenth house in Moss Landing someone died from the Big C. It had been true for Grammaw as well—stomach, guts rotted through to the core. Everyone knew the uranium dust that had been spewed into the atmosphere and now layered throughout the soil and water had done it, but what were a bunch of hillbillies gonna do? They had mortgages to pay and children to feed, certainly not the money it would take to prove a damn government-funded causality.

Truly dropped the last of her cigarette, *tzzz,* into the little bit of soda left in her Big Gulp. She sailed past the Moss Landing exit—now boasting two different Cincinnati chili places and a brand-new Taco Bell—toward the turn off where her childhood home sat tucked among a grove of ash trees.

Gravel popped under her tires as she rode up the long driveway. The house wasn't much to brag about—old and saggy siding, paint peeling in spots—but it had been home to several generations of Butcher women. And for Truly, it was a place of refuge, a place to go when everything had gone sideways, and all plans had failed. At least, it had been when Grammaw was alive. Now, Truly would be rooming with just her mother and that relationship was...complicated.

Truly parked and looked around before getting out of her car. She was back. Again. Dumped by some loser her mom had warned her about. Another cheater. Another asshole who wasn't worth the toilet paper she wiped her ass with.

Truly got out of the car and walked toward the house, the spongey, wet green of Southeastern Ohio this time of year, springing her feet forward. Elsewhere they called this time of day golden hour, but in these parts of the surrounding woods, the light always stayed a kind of gray-green. Calmness seeped through her skin. Her jaw unclenched, and she lowered her shoulders. No matter what, this was home, and a deep, bone-setting nostalgia did something to the back of her brain.

A bright red cardinal flitted among the branches encroaching the roof, and Truly thought spotting one might mean good luck. But then she noted all the spindly bareness, an anomaly this time of year. A lot of the trees in the area were dead or dying—had been for years now. Mourning woods, she called it. The larvae of the emerald ash borer ate them alive. Squirmy little fuckers would feed until they all died.

Her mom could've treated the trees, soil drenched the base with insecticide, but they'd already been told by every news outlet it was practically hopeless. The trees would die no matter what they tried, and if cancer didn't kill her mother, these might fall over and crush the house with her and Truly in it. Neither of them had any interest in calling a specialist to bring them down though. It would feel too much like they were desecrating graves. Let the mourning woods mourn, she thought.

As Truly made her way up the rickety front porch, she chose her steps carefully, because it sure as hell didn't seem like the rotting planks could support weight. The smell of browning hamburger wafted through the screen door, along with the chirpy delivery of the evening news.

Truly didn't bother knocking. She stepped inside and let the screen door slam behind her.

"Mom!" she called.

Beyond the living room, a shadow moved in the kitchen.

The metallic clank of pots and pans rang out. A wooden spoon clattered against the counter. Her mother cooked like a maniac, even when it was just those boxed meals with the cartoon glove mascot.

Truly grabbed the remote off the arm of the worn sofa, noting her mother's indentations in the cushions, and turned the TV off. She set her backpack near the hall that led upstairs to her old bedroom and walked toward the kitchen.

Her mother had a stereo going too, playing 1950s oldies, early doo-wap shit. Truly watched as her mother twirled and spun across the linoleum: stirring, tearing open the spice packet, dumping it in a pot and then winging it toward the trash can, little specks of who knew what sprinkling along the floor.

"Hey, Mom." Truly knew how her mother would react —the absolute drama of being interrupted—but also, she knew there was no way to avoid the spectacle, no matter how she greeted her mother.

"Oh! Sweet Jesus!" Her mom jumped like Truly knew she would. The spoon flew from her hand and landed with a *schmuck* on the counter. "Truly, honey, you scared the crap out of me! Living alone in these woods, I just don't have company." She clutched at where her heart should be.

"Mom, I called."

"Yes, but I didn't know *when* you'd be here!"

But Truly noticed the extra food she'd made and the table set for two. This was all part of one of her mother's performances, and Truly just went with it because why argue over something so stupid, so inconsequential. If her mother wanted to pretend to be frightened, well, who cared? The woman was probably pretty bored, living alone out here in the middle of nowhere.

What Truly couldn't ignore though, what stabbed her in the heart every time, was the look on her mother's face when she first glimpsed Truly. It was only a nano-second, a mere flicker behind the eyes, but it was there. And it was disgust.

Her mother hated hated hated Truly's body. It had started around puberty, when Truly's hips and ass grew wide. At least that's when Truly pinpointed it and started understanding that her own mother didn't approve of the way she looked, was embarrassed by her. But maybe it had been there from birth. Maybe she hated Truly's body for hijacking her own; who knew after this many years?

"Look at you!" her mother said, holding out her arms for a hug. "You've lost weight!"

"No, I haven't." Truly moved forward and hugged her mother, feeling how fragile, how insubstantial her skin and bones felt beneath her palms. "You have though." Truly regretted the words as soon as they moved past her lips. Her mother could live for weeks on those words alone. She was tiny, nothing more than a pine needle, and she employed all manner of *trends* to keep herself that way, including barely eating and chain smoking.

"Oh no! I'm as fat as ever." But the only thing anyone could have pinched on her was a tad bit of loose and wrinkling neck skin. "Dinner is almost done! And then we can sit and catch up."

"Do you need any help?" Truly asked, hoping she could just sit down.

"No, sit. Pour yourself some tea. Or wine. Whatever you want."

Truly chose the tea, not wanting to get tipsy with her mother and say a bunch of shit she really meant. Eloise, Elly for short, completed her little cooking dance and presented

Truly with a plate of glorified slop and a side salad of chopped iceberg lettuce. Truly took the plate, resignation over the whole scenario settling over her, and her mom chattered on about whatever town gossip she had fresh in her memory.

"You remember Tamara Faye, from down the road?"

Truly nodded. Of course she did. The Fayes had lived "down the road" her whole life. They were a burly bunch, prone to loud summer parties that ended with shotguns being fired into the canopy.

"Her son Brad—he went to school with you, didn't he—well, the FBI showed up here looking for him."

"The FBI? What for?"

Elly puckered her lips as if she'd just popped a lemon slice in her mouth. "Some *unsavory* pictures on his computer."

"If it was the FBI, then you mean like, kiddie porn. Jesus, Mom."

"Tamara marched right over here and told me he would never do such a thing, but he's gone. Nobody can find him."

"That's..." But Truly didn't know how to finish the sentence. It was disgusting to think someone she'd grown up with was straight up evil, but then was it really all that surprising? Brad had always been a fucking creep. When he'd shown up at high school parties, every girl knew to never be alone with him and never accept a drink from him. They'd joke about him being such a loser. But all along, real danger, real malice, had been right there. And they had just laughed.

"Horrible, Mom. That's really disgusting." Truly poked a fork into the mushy noodle mix on her plate.

"And Susan Parrish, one of my oldest friends. She owns the greenhouse down the way, remember?"

"Of course I do. She's basically family." Truly liked Susan

and never really understood why someone so cool liked hanging out with her mother, but they'd grown up together.

"Cancer."

Truly blew out a breath, then scooped more casserole into her mouth and chewed, even though she barely needed to. She could have just pressed the mush up against the roof of her mouth and swallowed. This is what coming home was always like, a constant doomscroll. Only instead of the news feeling distant and nebulous, it came for people Truly was actually familiar with and cared about. It left her feeling hollow and powerless.

"What kind?" Truly asked.

"Pancreatic." Elly's mouth formed a straight line. Everyone they'd known with pancreatic cancer had been a goner, and quickly.

"Is there anything good happening?" Truly asked, ignoring how her mother hadn't eaten anything.

Elly brightened, puffing a constant stream of cigarettes. She was well into her second glass of wine. "Well, yeah! Did ya see we got a Taco Bell?"

"Yeah, Mom. I saw it when I drove past the exit."

"You wouldn't even recognize downtown!"

Truly licked a speck of creamy hamburger off her back molar. Downtown hadn't ever been more than a strip of road that led to the high school, pig farms, and that defunct nuclear processing plant. They'd had a single pizza joint, a grocery store, and an antique "mall" but times, they were a'changing, even in Moss Landing.

"There's a flea market tomorrow. Wanna go?" Elly asked.

"Sure," Truly agreed. What else was she going to do? She scooped the last of her dinner into her mouth and offered to clean up.

"Are you gonna tell me what happened this time?" Elly asked.

Truly set her plate in the sink with a heavy *clink*. Her shoulders sagged. "It just didn't work out, Mom."

"Never does with you." Elly paused, took a long drag off her cigarette, then added, "I don't know why you think you'll ever keep a man, looking like ya do."

"There it is."

Her mother's words acted like a sugar spoon, scooping out tiny pieces of Truly's heart, her confidence, herself. Truly gripped the counter, gritting her teeth. Her mother's disdain wasn't usually vocalized until glass three of wine, but when she turned, she saw Elly pouring herself that third glass.

"Oh, don't look at me like that." Elly rolled her eyes. "I'm just being honest. That Phil was an asshole."

"I won't disagree with you about him."

"At the same time, it wouldn't kill ya to lose a little weight."

"And it wouldn't kill you to lay off the wine." Truly swiped the bottle from the table and headed out the back door.

"Hey! Bring that back!"

Outside, on the back porch, Truly heard her mom's chair scrape against the linoleum. She swigged from the bottle. The too-sweet punch on her tongue left her wanting nothing but water.

"Where do you think you're going?" Her mother's silhouette filled the screen door. Such a tiny fragile thing she was, who wielded way too much power over Truly.

"Just getting the hell away from you, Mom," Truly mumbled and turned away from her mother. She pounded down the porch steps that led to an overgrown garden and shed, then beyond to a trail into the woods.

"Don't be so sensitive," her mother growled. With the *click* of a lighter and the whoosh of her mom's breath of smoke, like some sentinel gust of wind, Truly was pushed further away.

She'd given up on the two of them having a *Gilmore Girls*-esque mother/daughter relationship a long-ass time ago. Still, Truly headed for the woods to clear her head. She hated being in the position of needing something from Elly. But what were her choices? She'd sold off her belongings and moved in with Phil early in their relationship. She had nothing now. He'd told her to quit her job and stay home to take care of the house, which she'd happily done, only to find out her cleaning was never good enough and her cooking was subpar. He asked her to change her hair color to blond and she'd obliged, the too-light strands falling in her eyes as she marched through the woods. She had to face it—she'd absolutely been his bitch. Phil had spotted her as an easy mark because that's exactly what she was. Truly wasn't as strong as she liked to think herself to be. Not as burly or non-conforming. She'd turned into an easy-bake Suzy Bundtcake without even questioning it.

When Truly stopped walking and looked up at the sky, evening had begun to fall in earnest and darkness spread under the canopy. Lightning bugs flickered all around, twinkling lights flashing green and yellow.

The mourning woods had always been a sanctuary for Truly, always been a place to get away from her mother, so she wasn't worried about getting lost. She could sleepwalk her way back, the muscle memory of those steps still strong. She let herself sink to the ground, and leaned against a tree trunk to watch the fireflies do their thing. She put her hands in the pockets of her hoodie and her fingers hit something slim and hard.

Yes! She pulled out her vape, set the mouthpiece on her lips and pressed the power button, hoping it was charged, hoping it had enough of something in there for one hit. It did. She inhaled, held her breath a few seconds, then blew it out. Just the ritual of the act brought calm.

She set her gaze toward the higher tree limbs and glimpsed the first twinkle of stars, knowing instinctively where they'd show up in the sky this time of year.

Home, somehow, felt both familiar and strange at the same time.

The black of night began to crowd her, and goosebumps broke out along her arms. Something, she couldn't put her finger on exactly what, felt unsafe. A twinge in the air, some bit of electricity or pheromone. The wanted neighbor could be out here, watching her, and her breath hitched in her throat at the thought. She poured out the rest of the wine, upturning the bottle. It would make a weapon if needed. It wasn't nothing.

The moss on which she sat began to glow a deep shade of teal, a darker, cooler shade than the lightning bugs. A tendril of what she thought might be a fern, hoped and begged was a fern, tickled her wrist.

"Fuck this," she spat the word and scrambled to a standing position. She shook her head, disbelieving what she'd felt, determined to stop scaring herself. Marching back toward her mother's house, she ditched her weed pen in the yard waste bin near the shed, then looked back at the forest.

The glow remained.

ENJOY THESE NOVELLAS IN ANY ORDER!

A HORDE OF DEAD POETS

Acknowledgments

I want to thank my Husband, Bobby, for not only giving me the kernel that sparked this story but for always listening to my ramblings as I searched for the right word. Jessica Moore, my partner in this new adventure that is Percy's Heart Press and for listening to my ramblings as I search for the right word. And Elle Beaumont for listening to my ramblings while I searched for the right word. This seems to have turned into a theme. I ramble too much. But you know what, it's all part of the process.

Seriously, though. There are so many great people in my life. The above three helped me with the story. And Jess had the patience of a saint or sailor (wink-wink) as I got the story down.

Writing can be a lonely endeavor, but it is one filled with infinite joy. Especially when I reach the end and smile at the work I've accomplished.

I want to send a special thank you to two amazing readers who always make me smile. Zarina and Tina. You both bring me so much joy and support. And Anthony (Zarina's hubby) I hope you enjoy this new Beatrice Monroe story!

I also want to thank my mother for believing in me and always asking how my writing is going. And the rest of my family who show so much love for my work.

And to you dear reader, I hope this story is an enjoyable one.

About C. Vonzale Lewis

C. Vonzale Lewis is the best-selling author of the Blood and Sacrifice Chronicles and various short fiction. She resides in Hesperia, CA where she spends her days plotting the demise of her enemies. All her stories tend to be dark with a little mystery thrown in and some love to round out the mix. When not writing, she enjoys reading, spending time with her husband, and binge-watching British crime fiction.

https://linktr.ee/authorcvonzalelewis

instagram.com/carlavlewis

Also by C. Vonzale Lewis

Blood & Sacrifice Chronicles

Lineage

Zealot

Tribe

Novellas:

Descendants of the Big House

Anthologies:

Flicker

Masks

Love on Main

Link by Link

Beyond the Cogs

Emporium of Superstition

This Fresh Hell

The Darkest Lullaby